Sisters

in Arms

Erica Ruppert

TREPIDATIO
PUBLISHING

ISBN: 978-1-950305-95-7 (sc)
ISBN: 978-1-950305-96-4 (ebook)
Library of Congress Control Number: 2021942746

First printing edition: July 23, 2021
Published by Trepidatio Publishing in the United States of America.
Cover Design: Don Noble | Layout: Scarlett R. Algee
Edited by Sean Leonard
Proofreading and Interior Layout by Scarlett R. Algee

Trepidatio Publishing, an imprint of JournalStone Publishing
3205 Sassafras Trail
Carbondale, Illinois 62901

JournalStone books may be ordered through booksellers or by contacting:
JournalStone | www.journalstone.com

For Brad, Bob, and Heather

Sisters
in Arms

I

MICHELLE shoved the letter back into her purse and rummaged around one-handed for her notebook. She kept her other hand tight on the steering wheel, and her eyes on the rutted road. There was no shoulder to pull over on, just grey sand drifting where the sea had lapped up to the edge of the pavement.

When she came to a crossroad, she stopped and put the car into park. She pulled the notebook out from under a rubber-banded stack of newspaper clippings and a battered book on Massachusetts history, then tossed her purse into the back seat.

She flipped through the soft and curling pages for the directions she had pieced together from old roadmaps. The remains of Ardoch should be huddled on the edge of Ipswich Bay, on the old coast road where it threaded away from Route 133 towards the wide Atlantic. The signpost at the eastern corner of the intersection was too faded to read, its paint scoured by years of sand and storms. She traced a finger over the sketch she had made. This should be the turn.

She made the right, her old Volkswagen juddering over the crumbled pavement. The road had not been kept up. So little traffic went between Ardoch and the rest of the world that it was no longer worth the effort.

Michelle was nearly certain that the Sisters of Providence were the only residents of Ardoch anymore. From what she had read in yellowed news clippings and the last few census reports, the town had been hit exceptionally hard by the flu sixty years ago, and any survivors had moved away long ago.

She was in the town before she realized it, surrounded by failing wooden structures. She downshifted, slowing the car to a crawl, looking around at the faded buildings and broken walls.

Suddenly, Michelle felt very lonely under the pale blue sky. She reached for the radio knob. Foreigner's "Double Vision" blared from the speakers, the guitars blurred with static. She jabbed at the preset buttons, but the car only filled with crackling voices and louder static. She turned the radio off.

Ardoch was behind her in only a few minutes. According to her notes, the Sisters of Providence lived in a mansion outside the town, closer to the bay. As Michelle nudged the car gently over a rise, she caught sight of the house.

It was a tall, rambling affair of grey shingle and peeling white trim, run down but not a ruin. Potted mums bloomed on the porch steps, bright yellow against the weathered wood. The yard in front of the house was clear, and Michelle pulled up close to the steps and parked.

Looking up through the windshield, she reached blindly into the back seat to grab her purse. Her hand closed on suede grown warm from sitting over the battery. She dug out her camera from a side pocket, hoping the heat hadn't damaged the film.

She got out of the car and snapped a few pictures of the house and its surroundings. The bay lay out of sight behind another set of low dunes. Scattered pines dotted a landscape of sand and tall grasses. Gulls called, invisible in the air, their cries softened by the wind blowing off the water.

Michelle tucked the camera into her pocket and straightened her coat as she climbed the steps to the front door. She paused, waiting to see if she had been seen. The sidelight windows were opaque with dirt, denying her a peek inside before she knocked.

The woman who opened the door was younger than Michelle, with long, untidy brown hair and a round face. She wore corduroys and a tight, long-sleeved jersey top printed with a paisley swirl.

"Hi," said Michelle. "I'm here to see Sister Adelia Cash?"

The woman's pale eyes flickered over Michelle.

"Miss Fortuna?" she said.

"Yes. No. I'm sorry. My name is de la Fortuna, not just Fortuna."

"Forgive me," the woman said.

"Perhaps it would be easier if you called me Michelle?"

Michelle shifted her purse to her shoulder and held out her hand. It was a long moment until the brown-haired woman took it in a soft grip and then quickly let it go.

"And you are?" Michelle asked.

"I'm Sister Cash. Adelia."

Michelle smiled quickly, a nervous tic. She shrugged out of her coat as she spoke, holding it against her chest.

"I'm sorry. I didn't know what to expect. You aren't easy to locate."

Adelia's expression did not change, but her eyes followed Michelle's movement.

"We're happier with our privacy. How did you find us, anyway?"

"My cousin lives up by Ipswich. You're a local legend. Almost like a ghost story."

Adelia held out her hand for Michelle's coat. Michelle paused before handing it over.

"Yes," Adelia said, draping the coat over the bannister. "It's been that way for a long time."

She stood for a second as if she did not know what to do next. She looked at Michelle, her expression neutral. "Come on in, then," she said.

She led Michelle into the parlor off the entryway, and gestured to a sagging green sofa set before the front windows. Michelle took in the decor. The easy chairs and side tables seemed to be a collection of thrift store finds, functional but mismatched. The walls were bare and in need of fresh paint.

"So, how much do you know about us? About what we do?" Adelia said, perching on the edge of the sofa next to Michelle.

Michelle dug her notebook out again, flipping through the pages as she spoke. "I know your group isn't affiliated with any church or particular faith tradition. I know the Sisters have been here since around the turn of the century, the 1910s or so. I know you take care of the cemetery here. Other than that, it's like I said. A ghost story."

From the back of the house came a clatter like falling pans. Adelia turned toward the noise, listening for a moment. Her brows knit into a frown. As the echoes stilled she turned back to Michelle.

"The Sisters have been here to watch over the island since Ardoch was abandoned. We couldn't just let it be forgotten."

Michelle pulled a pen from the notebook's spiral binding.

"But why? What's the reason behind your dedication? Why do you feel compelled to take care of the cemetery?"

"The Sisters of Providence were established as a retreat, to get away from the demands of society. Sister Letitia Eliot of the Boston Eliots bought this house in 1902 to have somewhere peaceful to go. Her cousin Alma joined her, and Alma's daughter Laurel. They brought in friends, and eventually a group of them lived here full-time."

Adelia's answer was well-rehearsed. She did not look at Michelle as she spoke. She got up and circled the room, still frowning, her attention elsewhere.

"Then in 1918, the town died. You know that much already. But the Sisters weren't affected, since they kept to themselves. There were probably twenty of them then. They took over burying the dead, and the people still left in town let them do it."

Michelle jotted notes as Adelia spoke.

"They called it the Baby Island then, didn't they?" Michelle asked. "Was it a potter's field?"

Adelia turned her pale eyes back to Michelle.

"No, not exactly," she said.

"I read," Michelle began, checking her notes, "that it was a burial ground for infants and small children. That adults were buried in the Gloucester cemeteries."

"Excuse me," Adelia said, as another crash came from the back of the house.

Michelle waited, picking at her nails. She looked around the room again, its shabbiness reminding her of old relatives. The front window let her see the ocean from where she sat.

From the back room came the sound of something wet dragging across the floor. A door slammed shut. Michelle jumped as Adelia walked quickly back into the parlor.

"It's all right," Adelia said. "An old house has its drafts."

———————◆———————

"Maybe you should see Ardoch first, before we get into the history too far. There's still time to walk through it today. Before dusk," Adelia said.

"I would appreciate that."

Adelia looked as if she wanted to say something more. The afternoon light made her pale eyes seem glassy.

But she said nothing. She handed Michelle back her coat, and plucked a poncho from the coat tree beside the door.

"It's only a little more than a mile," she said, and escorted Michelle out of the house. A salty wind struck them as they stepped onto the porch.

"Should we drive?" Michelle asked.

Adelia did not answer. She strode heavily across the sandy yard and up to the road without looking back to see if Michelle was behind her. Michelle decided she hadn't heard the question over the wind. She caught up with Adelia, and walked with her in silence until they reached the eastern edge of Ardoch.

Michelle whistled through her teeth as they followed the pitted road through the remains of the town. Even though she had seen it from her car, being in the midst of the empty houses was different. She took pictures as they walked, documenting the loss.

Ardoch had all but dried up and blown away. Most of the buildings were ruins, collapsed and rotted away. What was left of Ardoch reminded Michelle of driftwood piled up in a cove. The town had never been more than a loose cluster of twenty or twenty-five houses and outbuildings, home to a few families who wanted their privacy. Now it was splinters and waste.

Adelia led Michelle down the single cross street, and then circled Ardoch's former town limits. Michelle estimated the entire town was no more than five or six blocks wide, using an urban measure, and maybe seven blocks long.

"Can we go inside any of them?" Michelle asked.

Adelia shook her head.

"It wouldn't be safe," she said. Michelle nodded.

As the women turned back toward the Sisters' house, Michelle slowed her pace.

"Adelia?" she asked. "What brought you here?"

Adelia gazed off over Michelle's head. "I grew up south of Hamilton. I heard about it. Like you said, it's a local legend. I drove up a couple of years back to check it out, and ended up talking with Sister Akady. It seemed like the right thing to do."

She shrugged, and looked around at the shell of Ardoch.

"Not much else to see here, unless you want to circle around again. I wouldn't. It's getting late."

"Let's head back, then, I guess," Michelle said.

By the time they reached the house again the sun was far behind them. The night seemed to spill in from the ocean, washing over the surf and the sand.

"You should stay," Adelia said. "The roads are bad, especially in the dark. We can get an early start tomorrow. I can show you the island."

Michelle paused. She hadn't planned on an overnight stay.

Adelia watched her. "It will give you a chance to read through some of the books we have here, on local history. On the Sisters."

Adelia's persistence was more eager than threatening. "Okay," Michelle said at last.

"Good. Wait in the parlor for now. I'll get us some supper."

Michelle chose to sit in an old brown wing chair that faced the uncovered windows. Moonlight flickered on the waves in the bay. The play of light was broken by a black area some distance from the shore. She thought it must be the island. The sky and the sea filled the room with their dark presence. She wished there were curtains to draw.

After a long while Adelia came back with a tray holding two bowls of tomato soup, a sleeve of crackers, and two glasses of milk. Tucked under her arm were a few books so old their spines had peeled away. She let the books fall to the floor as she placed the tray on the coffee table. She nudged them toward Michelle with her toe, almost coy.

Michelle picked the tumbled books up. She flipped one open, an ancient cloth-bound thing with fragile, yellow pages that crumbled as she turned them.

"To the Sea," she read aloud. "A Seaman's Recollections."

"Yes," Adelia said. "That one talks about a bunch of weird phenomena a sailor encountered in these waters. The other one is more a memoir by one of the Ardoch people from the 1870s. Clarent. I don't think the family survived the flu. The third is another memoir."

"Thank you," Michelle said. She took her bowl of soup and crumbled a handful of crackers into it.

They both ate quickly, in silence.

As Michelle sipped the last of her milk, Adelia said, "I know you have a family history here, too. You mentioned it in one of your letters."

Michelle dabbed her mouth with a paper napkin.

"Not much of a history, really. More an old family story. An anecdote."

She paused, then leaned forward.

"My great-grandfather was a fisherman, mostly, out of Gloucester. But my father told me that one day he saw something in the water, something he didn't have the words to describe, except that it was black and scaley and had the face of a man. And it scared him so much he never went to sea again."

Adelia put her bowl down and leaned forward as well. Michelle felt as if she were telling a campfire story.

"It wasn't long after that he moved the family from Gloucester to Passaic, New Jersey," Michelle continued. "He had a sister there. My father said even then he complained about the river, though he thought it was fouled enough that it would be safe."

Adelia dared to put her hand on Michelle's arm. "Was it?"

"Was it what?" Michelle said, brushing away the unwanted contact.

"Was it safe?"

———— ♦ ————

Adelia gave Michelle an upstairs bedroom for the night. Adelia brought up towels and a toothbrush for her, and a tiny bar of hotel soap. She showed her the bathroom at the end of the hall, past three more closed doors. Michelle got the impression that she would have the second floor entirely to herself.

After washing up she looked around the bedroom, resigned. It was spare, and not too dusty, and furnished like an old motel room. But there were extra blankets for the bed and a portable radio on the windowsill. It would do for a night.

She leaned back against the wooden headboard, lit a cigarette, and blew smoke rings toward the ceiling. The ashtray on the nightstand was a souvenir novelty from Boston, with a waving lobster painted on the bottom. She tapped her ashes onto the creature's smiling face.

The house was surprisingly quiet. The only sounds she heard were the muted lap of the ocean and her own breathing. She got up and turned on the radio, spinning the dial. The stations she could pull in sounded as distant as the moon. She turned the radio off, opened the window a few inches, and listened to the waves.

She looked at her wristwatch. It was just past nine, too early for her to sleep.

The books Adelia had given her were too decayed to bother with, in her mood. She turned back the first few leaves of the top one, feeling the paper crumble under her fingertips, sentences broken into fragments as the pages broke apart. She had no patience for their age and fragility. She put the books aside and got out her notes, spreading them out on the bed.

Michelle had narrowed her master's thesis to the 1918 influenza pandemic's effect on the small towns of the New England coast, then narrowed it even further to the handful of towns that had never recovered, and then at last to lonely Ardoch in Massachusetts.

While cities large and small had suffered, Ardoch was the only one that made Michelle think of the folk stories about the Black Plague, of whole towns dead and forgotten, lost until some outsider stumbled upon them. In Ardoch, the flu swept through and killed off more than a third of the small population. Entire families died. The bodies were left to rot until the few survivors became brave or disgusted enough to collect and bury them. The dead went into a communal grave, shrouded and barely mourned. Ardoch was soon abandoned. Sixty years later, the town was a memory with a few stragglers still clinging to what had been.

The Sisters of Providence.

Why don't they leave? Michelle wrote in the page margin. *There's no one left. What are they waiting for?*

---◆---

Michelle woke at first light, disoriented by the unfamiliar space. She had not slept well, with washes of vague dreams rupturing her rest. Her notes were scattered across the floor where they had fallen. After a moment she calmed down, pulled on her clothes against the chill in the room, and gathered the papers into an untidy pile that she shoved back into her bag.

She walked down the stairs carefully, hoping for silence, but the steps squeaked beneath her weight. She could not hear any other movement in the house. At the bottom of the staircase she crossed the entryway and checked the front door. It was securely locked. Hazy daylight seeped in through the dirty sidelights.

Michelle turned down the hallway toward the back rooms of the house. On one side of the hall was a shuttered dining room, dim and barren. Across from it was the kitchen, its door ajar. She pushed the door open and peered in.

The room was clean, except for an overturned garbage pail and a long smear of some dark fluid across the scuffed yellow linoleum near the back door. The back door itself listed inward, its upper hinge twisted out of place. A wooden table was pushed up against the door to keep it closed. Michelle stepped in. The faint smell of salt and old seaweed filled the room. She backed out, and pulled the door closed behind her.

She went back to the parlor. Adelia was there, awake and bundled on the sofa in a crocheted afghan.

"Are you ready?" Adelia said.

Michelle paused, surprised.

"I never heard you get up. Are we the only ones here?" Michelle asked.

"Yes. But it's all right," Adelia said as she unwrapped herself. She was already dressed. "We have to watch the tides. It's best we get going."

———— ◆ ————

They followed a rough footpath toward the bay, walking straight toward the rising sun. Michelle stopped as they reached the beach to look back over the low slope of the dunes at the house's sharply peaked roof. Sun glinted off the upper windows in bright sparks. Adelia followed her gaze.

"It's been here a long time," Adelia said. "Lots of storms, but none have washed it away so far."

She turned and kept walking.

They crossed a few more yards of sand, to where a paved causeway stretched out into the water. The graveyard had been made on an island in the bay, perhaps a quarter mile out.

"This is it," Adelia said, and climbed up the rocks to the weathered pavement.

Michelle stepped carefully onto the eroded causeway, following Adelia closely. The tide was turning, starting to come in. She could see the pale glitter of sand where it filled the cracks between the black rocks, the remains of other tides. The sea fell away in grey depths on either side of the rocks, how far down she couldn't guess. She didn't think it could be so deep so close to shore. Along the sloping sides of the causeway, strings of dark orbs in gelatinous casings floated on the rising tide. The orbs were the size of oranges within their milky, protective slime.

"What are these?" Michelle called to Adelia, a tremor in her voice.

Adelia stood with her back to her.

"Eggs," she said. "Did you read anything in those books?"

"I couldn't concentrate," Michelle said.

Adelia nodded, and kept walking.

The island, when they reached it, was little more than a wide flat rock pushed up from the sea bed, battered and cracked and weathered into sharp angles. Sand had covered it thickly enough that some stubborn weeds had rooted. Michelle walked slowly around the small island, looking at the three lines of grey stones that marked communal graves. The back of the graveyard had crumbled into the sea, and the long trenches there had been scoured clean of their sad contents long ago. A sign stood, canted at an angle, the inscription faded to a ghost of lettering. Michelle squinted at it, thinking it said, "our beloved children." She couldn't be sure. She snapped a picture.

Adelia came to stand beside her.

"The island is higher than high tide," she said. "But there's no escaping it."

Michelle moved away from her. The ocean was different here than at the New Jersey shore, greyer, hungrier, too willing to swallow her up. She remembered her childhood summers, playing in the sand beneath a bright sun and the waves lapping up over the holes she dug. Not here. Here the waves would crash down upon her like a falling mountain and drive her deep into the broken cobble. She stepped away from the crumbling edge, forcing her attention back to the graves.

"What do you tend here?" Michelle said, loud enough for Adelia to hear her above the surf.

"Nothing, really."

Michelle pushed her hair out of her eyes as she turned toward Adelia again.

"But I thought that was the Sisters' purpose, to tend the graves."

"It hasn't been for years now. Since before I came."

"But then why are you still here?"

Adelia smiled shyly. She turned her pale eyes toward the ground.

"You saw how empty the house is," she said. "I'm the last Sister of Providence. Joan, Ellena, Liz, they're all gone." Adelia looked up. "I need help out here. When you kept writing letters, I began to hope you would be interested enough to be willing to help me. That's why I let you come."

Michelle was suddenly wary of this strange woman, suddenly awake to the mistake of being alone with her in this desolate place. She gripped her own arms to stop her trembling.

Adelia noticed.

"Don't be afraid of me," she said. "I know I sound nuts. But I'm not. And I know that's what I would say, if I was nuts."

Adelia knelt beside the long mound of a grave and scraped away the sandy soil with her blunt fingers.

"Here," she said. "Look at this."

A few inches beneath the surface nestled a buried bundle. The wrappings were leached of colour and rotted away, but the thing half-hidden within them glistened and pulsed. Adelia plucked at the shredded fabric until Michelle could see the sheer chitinous sheen of skin, the soft throb of a heart within its casing. Michelle realized it was not fabric that wrapped the thing, but dead tissue.

Adelia dug it out and held it up toward her.

Michelle leaned toward it despite herself, fascinated. She cupped her own hands around the amber shell Adelia held. Warmth seeped through, into her palms. Inside the casing, a primordial creature turned, slithering against its confines.

"What is it?" she whispered.

"It's their larva. It's why we're here. This is when they're vulnerable," Adelia said, her voice soft and urgent.

"Vulnerable," Michelle repeated, tasting the word. "But what is it?"

"We can't get them when they're in the water," Adelia went on, past her question. "We have to wait until they hatch, and go into their second form."

"What second form?"

"They pupate. They burrow after they hatch. Then we can dig them out. I wish you had read the books. They explain it better than I can."

Michelle let go of the amber pupa and stood up. Adelia still crouched like a supplicant with the pulsing thing in her hands.

"What happened to Sister Akady?" Michelle asked.

Adelia looked past Michelle to watch the waves. "She had to leave our house, she had to go home. Not everyone lasts. They're not all strong enough."

"What do you mean?"

"There are sacrifices to living here. Responsibilities."

"Like what? Can you tell me?"

Adelia smiled again, a crack in the moon of her face. And then she crushed the amber shell between her hands, twisting the thing within until it was jelly.

"Oh my God. What are you doing?" Michelle cried out.

"This is why I'm still here," Adelia said, pleading. "Why I need your help. These things need to eat once they emerge. Do you get it? It wasn't the flu that ended Ardoch."

Adelia dropped the mess she held and stood up, wiping her hands on her pants.

Michelle retched, and stepped to the edge of the island as she spat out bile. Looking out over the choppy grey sea, she squinted at something sleek and black slicing through the waves toward the shore. She thought it was a seal at first, until it came closer and she saw it was not a seal at all. She turned away before she could see a face, and sprinted toward the causeway.

Behind her, Adelia screamed defiance and followed.

Michelle stumbled across the broken pavement and ran up the beach to the house. She tugged her keychain from her coat pocket and threw herself into her car. Adelia came over the dunes only seconds behind her and ran into the house.

Michelle pulled out in a spray of sand, driving too fast for the state of the road. Then Ardoch was behind her, and she was back on the coast road. She shifted gears, speeding up as the road curved close against the water.

A black form rose up from the lapping water and slithered onto the road in front of her. This time, Michelle saw its face.

She hit the brakes hard, and the VW's tires juddered across the broken pavement as the car skipped sideways. The engine stalled. Michelle shrieked as she stomped on the clutch and brake and wrested the gear shift into neutral. She looked up, but the road before her was empty. Movement flickered at the corner of her eye. She turned the key so hard she thought she might break it, but the old car coughed and turned over. She threw it into gear again and drove.

The sea sucked at the edge of the pavement on this stretch, chewing it away. Michelle bit down her panic. She did not glance at the waves. She would not look to see what washed up with them.

II

"YOU can't be serious," Irene said, stuffing a pillow into its case. "It rattled you enough that you hid in a motel for two days before coming here, and you want to go back?"

Michelle sat at the foot of the bed, picking at the pink chenille spread.

"Yeah, but I have to," she said. "I needed to think about it before I did anything. I swear I saw something in Ardoch, and I want to go back and see if it was real. Besides, I left my stuff there when I peeled out. My thesis notes, research. My purse. Stuff I can't just replace."

Irene fluffed the pillow and tossed it onto the bed. She sat down next to Michelle and tugged gently at her cousin's thick ponytail.

"Look," she said with a smirk. "If it's that bad in New Jersey, you know you can stay here for a couple of months."

"That's not it, Irene, and you know it," Michelle said, brushing her hand away from her hair. "Dad's been weird ever since Mom died. He's afraid of losing me, too. He gets really over-protective." She paused. "But I don't have any problem at home that I want to run away from."

She got up and looked at herself in the mirror above the dresser in order to watch Irene in the reflection. Irene flopped back across the bed and kicked her feet back and forth.

"You sure about that? Because I've got plenty of problems I want to run from."

"Like what? You have the job, the boyfriend, the cool parents. Spill."

Irene sat up.

"Matt wants to get married," Irene said. "He wants a bunch of kids."

"I didn't know it was that serious."

Irene craned her neck and grinned. "Neither do my folks. They want me to go to school before I get married."

Michelle shook her head. "And my dad wants me to stop with school already and settle down. Seriously, though. Don't you want to marry him?"

"I don't know," Irene said, her smile fading. "I don't know if I'm ready for it. With him, at any rate."

Michelle turned around to face Irene. "Drive up to Ardoch with me. We can talk. You can get your mind off things."

Irene smiled again.

"You know you sound goofy. You sound like you believe in the Creature from the Black Lagoon."

"If you'd been there, you'd know what I mean," Michelle said. "When I go back, I'd really like it if you came with me."

Irene continued kicking her feet.

"If I'd seen something wild enough to make me run away, I don't think I'd be going back," she said to the ceiling. "Even if my stuff was still there."

Michelle sat down next to her cousin.

"Come with me when I go to Fotomat later. I want you to see what I'm talking about."

———◆———

Michelle pulled away from the kiosk and into a parking spot, opened the envelope, and flipped through the photographs. She handed Irene the shots of the house and the dunes, but Irene only glanced at them and put them down on her lap. The pictures of Ardoch's decay elicited a grunt of interest.

"Yeah, it looks like the kind of place kids would go to scare themselves," she said.

Michelle nodded. "It does. But there was no sign that they do. There was no graffiti, no empty beer cans, no campfires."

She looked at the photographs still in her hand.

"It didn't occur to me until just now. There isn't anything like that out there. The town, the house, the island, they're all just left alone."

Irene shrugged. "Maybe it's not worth the trip."

"You lived out here the whole time. Didn't kids from your school go out there for fun?"

Irene gazed through the windshield at the flow of people going in and out of the supermarket. She shook her head.

"Nah. It wasn't cool."

Michelle watched her cousin's profile until Irene returned her stare.

"Here, check out this one," Michelle said, handing Irene the picture of the graves on the island.

"Lovely," Irene said.

"Don't be nasty," Michelle said. "This is where they buried the babies, after the flu epidemic."

Irene shook her head.

"I really don't know why you want to go back out there."

Michelle examined the prints in her hands. She lingered over the one of the dunes.

"It's only a few miles from here, but it's like another world. Everyone left it behind."

She laughed flatly.

"It's funny to see what happens to a social structure when a sudden event...removes a portion of the group."

Irene's mouth quirked into not quite a smile. "There's that degree again."

Michelle ignored the dig.

"We're used to thinking about towns and villages being wiped out by disease in the Middle Ages or in Third World countries, but it has always happened, everywhere," she said. "Whenever they discovered a new country, the native population died off in droves. And the same thing happened here, with the influenza pandemic in 1918. It wiped a few American towns clean off the map. Ardoch was one."

Irene was quiet for a moment, then reached over and slapped Michelle's leg.

"Enough of all this fun discussion," she said. "Let's get some pizza and go home."

———— ◆ ————

A sharp knock sounded on Irene's bedroom door.

"What, Dad?" Irene said loudly.

"Is Michelle with you?"

"Yeah." Irene got up and swung open the door.

"Hi, Uncle Pauly," Michelle said. "You weren't home when I got here or I would have said hi right away."

She went to him and held out her open arms, but he held up a warning finger.

"Your dad is looking for you," he said. "He called your aunt at work. He's worried."

Michelle reached out and hugged her uncle as he spoke.

"He's always worried, Uncle Pauly. I'll call him."

Paul pushed her back to look into her face.

"No, honey. You need to tell him you're on your way home, and then get there. He's sick with the flu and needs help. You know he wouldn't have bothered your Aunt Suzy otherwise."

Michelle nodded, suddenly grave.

"And you," Paul said, looking at his daughter. "When your cousin shows up out of the blue, you let us know, okay?"

Irene grinned at him as he left the room.

Michelle looked at her.

"Okay, I gotta go," she said. "Thanks for the change of clothes. I'll get them back to you."

"No problem," Irene answered.

Michelle opened the door and stepped out into the hall.

"But please, think about coming with me when I go up to Ardoch," she said, and pulled the door closed behind her.

III

MICHELLE got home as dusk was falling, the sky slowly going dark. She pulled into the driveway and let herself in the kitchen door.

The house was quiet. The kitchen was its usual controlled mess, with dishes in the sink and a pot on the stove. She lifted the lid to find chicken noodle soup. It was still warm. She put the pot in the fridge and went upstairs to check on her father.

His bedroom door stood open. She stepped into the dimly lit room, wrinkling her nose at the tang of sweat and vomit in the air. Her father lay curled up in the dirty blankets, asleep. She picked up the bowl he had used to throw up in and went quietly back downstairs.

She wrapped the whole bowl in a couple of plastic bags and put it outside on the back steps. She washed the dishes, then checked the refrigerator for dinner supplies. There was the soup, a Corningware half-full of leftover spaghetti, and some sliced cheese.

It felt like she'd been gone more than six days.

She smelled the spaghetti. It was still good. That would be her dinner, at least until she got to the grocery store.

She called Irene to let her know she was home, then went to the front of the house to turn on the living room lights against the gathering autumn dark.

A stack of four letters had been separated from the pile of mail on the hall table, all addressed to her. They were from Adelia. Upstairs, she heard her father groan, and the bed squeak as he rolled over.

"Dad?" she called. She held still for a moment, listening, but he didn't answer.

She turned on the hall light and opened the first letter in the stack.

October 8, 1978
Dear Michelle,

I know you have no reason to come back to Ardoch, but I would appreciate it if you would.

There is still a great deal you could learn about the town and its history, and about the Sisters. And as I said last week, I need help.

I have your things here. They are safe and waiting for you, if you come back for them.

If not I can mail them back to you.

But I hope you will come.

Sister Adelia Cash

Michelle tucked the letter back into its envelope and opened the next.

October 9

Dear Michelle,

Please consider coming back to Ardoch and the Sisters. Consider it a personal favor to me.

I know I am not in a position to ask you for favors, but I need your help.

Yours,

Sr. Adelia Cash

She skipped the third letter and opened the last one, postmarked a day ago.

October 9

Dear Michelle,

Please come soon. I need your help.

Yours,

Adelia.

Either Adelia had lost track of the days, or she had written three letters in quick succession.

Michelle stuffed the letters back in their envelopes and shoved them into her back pocket before she opened the front door to check for today's mail.

In the bundle she pulled from the mailbox was yet another letter from Adelia. She sighed, and added everything to the pile.

Her father's voice drifted down from above. "Michelle? Is that you?"

"Yeah, Dad," she said, running up the stairs into the gloom.

She turned on the small bedside lamp rather than the overhead light. In the soft glow her father looked ghostly pale.

"Hi, baby," he said to her as he struggled to lift his head.

"How long have you been sick, Daddy?"

He coughed and winced. "Couple of days. My head hurts. Everything hurts."

Michelle went to the hall bathroom and wet a washcloth to wipe his face with. "You made soup before?"

"Yeah. Couldn't eat it."

She smoothed his hair back with the damp cloth.

"All right. I'm going to go heat a little up for you now. Just rest. I'll take care of things."

He father turned his head with great effort, his bleary eyes half-shut.

"You sound just like your mother," he said.

Michelle shook her head slightly, embarrassed.

"But you do. She always said you were turning out just like her."

He coughed again.

"Did you know you were born in a caul?"

Michelle met his eyes. "A caul? Like, second sight?"

"Yeah, like that." He laughed. "You looked like you were wrapped in Saran wrap. Did you ever figure out how to tell the future?"

Michelle smiled slowly. "No. Got too busy with school."

"I miss your mother so much," he said, his voice rough with mucus. "She needed the ocean. She never got there enough."

"I remember going down the shore," Michelle said. "We used to go all the time. I remember Mom swimming way out."

Mike coughed. "It wasn't enough."

Michelle pressed her hand to his cheek.

"Enough talking, Dad. You've got a good fever going. I'm going to get you that soup now."

She left the room before he could answer her.

———◆———

It was after eleven before Michelle was sure her father was as settled as he could be. She crawled into her own bed, exhausted but too worried to sleep.

Across the hall, she heard her father grunt and cough. His breathing was loud, but steady.

She pulled her blankets tight around her and stared at the curtained window. A car rumbled by in the street below. Rising heat clinked in the radiators.

She wished Adelia had a phone. She rehearsed what she would say to her if she could just make a call, as she fell, at last, asleep.

———————◆———————

In the morning, Michelle called the university to tell her advisor she would not be back this semester. She told him that her thesis had taken an unexpected turn, and that she needed more time. He listened politely, wished her well, and transferred her back to his secretary to discuss the withdrawal paperwork. Michelle asked the woman to mail anything that needed her signature. She would not be coming back to campus anytime soon.

Then she called her job at the Grand Union and with a feigned rasp told them she had the flu, and wasn't sure when she would be back.

Freed from her outside commitments, Michelle settled into a new routine in the house. When her father was awake, she catered to him. When he slept, she went through the drawer in the dining room sideboard where all the family pictures had ended up. The monotony of the old photos was soothing.

She stacked a few of the little red photo booklets on the cluttered dining table and flipped through them. Her mother had always meant to put their pictures in real albums, but had never gotten to it. Each booklet had slots for twenty-four snapshots, and most of them were filled. Michelle smiled at the familiar pictures of herself as a child, mementoes of the holidays she spent with Irene, Uncle Pauly, and Aunt Susan. One booklet had the faded record of the winter she and Irene were nine, when it snowed for Christmas and the girls spent the day outside, cold, wet, and happy.

But the posed family shots made her sad. They always looked to her as if everyone was waiting for something that never came.

Tucked into a folder were some loose photographs, odd sizes that didn't fit into the four-by-six booklets. She didn't remember these as well as the others, although she knew she must have seen them. They were all pictures of her mother, young and smiling into the sun on various beach outings.

One was paper-clipped to a folded sheet of notebook paper. She did not recognize the photo.

She unclipped it from the paper, and unfolded the sheet to reveal her mother's fine, looping handwriting.

God, do I miss going down the shore. But the gas prices, the lines— even Sandy Hook is too far. Mike keeps saying we can retire down to Toms River, but that's years away. I miss the ocean now.

Michelle stared at the lined sheet, wondering why she hadn't ever read it before. She was sure she had gone over everything in the wide, deep drawer more than once.

She refolded the paper and put it aside. She studied the faded photo of her mother, her pants rolled up, standing in the waves. There was no denying the resemblance. She had her mother's wide-set amber eyes and generous mouth, her pinched chin and straight brown hair. She flipped the picture over. "Ana, Seaside 1961."

Michelle remembered how often her mother took her down the shore. Her father didn't join them most of the time—he didn't like the long drive, the crowds, or the inescapable sand. But her mother would take her at least once a month in all but the coldest months, and if they did not swim they would take off their shoes and wade in the shallows. Michelle remembered standing still and letting the swirling waves bury her feet in the sand.

She remembered the year she turned seventeen, when her father was out of work for a while and they couldn't afford to go down the shore anymore. That was the year her mother got sick, and never recovered. She died the following year, at the height of summer.

Michelle hadn't gone to the beach since then.

But now the cold Massachusetts coast drew her, as the New Jersey shore had drawn Ana. She looked down at the picture in her hands, and started to cry.

After nursing him through more than a week of bed rest, Michelle found her father in the kitchen one morning making coffee and toast.

"Are you up for this, Dad?" she asked.

"I'm here, so I'm up for it," he said. "Do you want breakfast?"

Michelle got the plastic pitcher of orange juice out of the refrigerator. "Sit down, Dad. I'll make it."

He looked at her for a long moment, then sat. He had lost weight, and his face was drawn and sagging despite his attempt at heartiness.

Michelle buttered the toast and set it in front of her father. She poured him a glass of juice and poured milk into his coffee. "Do you want any eggs?"

"No. I'm not quite ready for eggs yet," he said.

Michelle got her own coffee and sat across from him.

"I called the plant, and told them I'd be back tomorrow," he said.

Michelle looked at him sharply. "Why don't you just finish out this week and start fresh on Monday?"

Mike coughed and waved his hand at her.

"How long do you think I can afford to be out of work?" he said when he caught his breath. "I'm lucky Tony likes me."

Michelle just shook her head. "You're stubborn."

"Yeah," he said.

She drained her coffee cup.

"You haven't been going to work, either," he said.

She shook her head. "No."

He reached across the table and gripped her hand. "What are you doing, Shelly?"

She gently pulled her hand away.

"I've been thinking, a lot. About life. About Mom."

Mike sat back in his chair. "And?"

She sighed. "I think I need to go back up to Massachusetts for a while. Do some real research on Mom's side up there."

She met her father's eyes. He looked very old, grey and unshaven and wrapped in his striped terrycloth robe.

"I don't like the idea of you going off alone, Shelly. There are too many crazy people out there."

Michelle tapped a cigarette out, lit it, and took a long drag.

"Dad," she said, "they got Son of Sam already. And the Manson family. I'm not stupid. I'll be fine."

He held out his hand for her cigarette and took a shallow puff. He coughed the smoke back out.

"Look," she said as he regained his breath. "I asked Irene if she'll come with me. I'll call her and get an answer before I go, okay?"

He paused.

"Okay," he said. "Now would you clean this mess up? I have to start bracing for work tomorrow."

He got up slowly, put his coffee cup in the sink, and headed back upstairs. Michelle ate the cold toast and listened to his lagging footsteps over her head.

———————◆———————

Michelle stayed in bed late the next morning, listening to her father slowly get ready and leave the house. She waited until she heard him pull out of the driveway before she got up and padded downstairs.

The stack of mail accumulating on the hall table had slipped and scattered across the floor. As Michelle gathered up the flyers and envelopes, she saw how many letters Adelia had sent. She pulled them out and threw them away.

She dug out her box of stationery from the junk drawer and sat at the messy kitchen table.

Dear Sister Cash, Michelle wrote. *I will be back up to see you by early next week at the latest. I'm sorry I cannot be more exact. I have some ends to tie up here before I can leave.*

That was enough, she thought. No need for details. That she would return at all was plenty.

———————◆———————

Michelle called Irene, but no one answered. She realized they must all be at work. It hadn't taken long for her to lose her bearings without a regular schedule.

Now that she had decided to leave again, she began nesting. She cleaned the house while her father was at work, even washing the kitchen walls to clean the residue of cigarette smoke from them. He fussed at her when he got home, but stayed out of her path over the weekend. She did all the laundry she could find. She cleaned her room. She went grocery shopping, and cooked and froze a few meals for him.

Then she packed what clothes and other things she thought she would need for at least a couple of weeks, and left a message with her aunt to tell Irene she would be there tomorrow.

As she was packing her car in the early morning, her father came out the kitchen door with an old cardboard box in his arms.

"Michelle," he said. "Take these with you."

"What are they?" she asked, taking the burden from him.

"Your mother's stuff. Her family stuff," he said. "I want you to take her notebooks with you. There might be something there you would like to know. It might help you figure things out. She was always scribbling things down. She wanted to be a writer, but she didn't have time, what with working and taking care of you and the house. Bring them back when you're done."

"Thanks," she said, sliding the box onto the back seat.

As she straightened up he caught her in a fierce hug.

"Bring them back," he said.

"I will, Dad," she said. "When I'm done."

IV

IRENE pulled open the front door as Michelle came up the walk.
"You just can't stay away," Irene said by way of greeting.
"Nope," Michelle answered, handing Irene her valise.

Irene pulled her cousin into the warmth of the house.

"Are your folks home?" Michelle asked. She didn't want to slight her uncle again.

"They're both at work," Irene answered, leading Michelle upstairs.

"Great. Where's your suitcase?"

Irene stopped and glared at her cousin.

"I said I'd think about it, Michelle."

The phone rang in the kitchen, and Michelle had to press against the wall as Irene rushed down past her to grab it.

Michelle continued upstairs to leave her valise in Irene's room before quietly picking her way back down. She tiptoed through the dining room and pushed the swinging door gently open. Irene's eyes flicked to her and then down at the floor.

"Matt," Irene said urgently into the receiver. "Shut up and listen. I am not ready for this."

She was quiet for a moment, then raised her voice.

"No. No. No. I am not going to get over anything. We want different things—that doesn't make either of us wrong. I love you, but I'm not ready for what you want right now."

She wrapped the phone cord around her hand. "Then I guess it is. Yes. I'm sorry, Matt. I'm sorry. Goodbye."

Irene hung up, and sighed.

Michelle looked everywhere but at her cousin. She went to the sink and pretended to dry the dishes piled on the drainboard.

"Are you okay?" she said to her hands, wiping a bone-dry plate.

Irene sighed again and sat down. She picked at a tear in the vinyl tablecloth, pulling out strands of the fleece backing.

"Yeah. This has been coming for a while," she said, watching her own busy fingers. "Now's as good a time as any, what with a road trip planned."

Michelle turned and put her hand on Irene's shoulder, squeezing gently.

"I didn't know all this was going on, or I wouldn't have pushed you. I'm sorry."

"It's okay. I didn't tell you," Irene said, standing up and moving away from her cousin. "Might as well get out of here for a while. I have a few days off from work anyway. Give me a little while to pack."

Michelle stayed in the kitchen when Irene went upstairs. She made a couple of cheese sandwiches for the road while she waited.

She thought she heard Irene's muffled crying overhead, but when Irene came back down her eyes were clear. She had a tote bag slung over her shoulder and a pair of sneakers dangling from her hand.

"Ready as I'll ever be," Irene said.

Michelle put the sandwiches in a paper bag and threw in a couple of apples from a bowl on the counter.

"Did you tell your folks you're going with me?"

"No. I'll call them when we get there."

"Can't. The Sisters don't have a phone. Leave them a note."

With another sigh, Irene scribbled something on a piece of scrap paper next to the phone and tucked the slip under the sugar bowl on the table.

"Let's go," she said.

———•·———

The drive from the outskirts of Ipswich to the ruins of Ardoch was only an hour long, but it was a distance that brought Michelle and Irene from one reality to another. The crowded town gave way to desolate coastal roads and the sense of having left something important behind.

Irene slouched in her seat, her eyes on the sky. Michelle tried to keep up a stream of light conversation, but Irene responded slowly and without interest. The drive felt far longer than it should. Michelle gripped the wheel and stared straight ahead as Irene withdrew further into her own shell.

As they got near the turnoff from Route 133, Michelle tried again.

"Look," she said. "We're going to be there pretty soon. Are you going to snap out of it, or am I going to have to bring you home and come back alone?"

Irene turned to face her cousin.

"Wow," she said. "How about, 'Thanks for coming'? How about, 'I'm sorry you and Matt broke up'?"

Michelle shifted gears as she slowed on the uneven pavement.

"I'm sorry," she said after a moment. "Thank you. I am really glad you're along. And I am really sorry about you and Matt."

Irene turned away again. She breathed onto the window glass, and scratched a doodle into the patch of fog.

"I want to get married eventually, have a couple of kids," she said. "But I want to live a little first. Matt's the first guy I've been serious about, but he's in such a rush."

Michelle glanced sideways at Irene, glad she was talking.

"Maybe it will work itself out," she said. "Maybe he'll lighten up."

The car shuddered as the road crumbled beneath them. They were entering Ardoch. Irene looked at the ruins in silence. Michelle kept her eyes on the road as they crested the rise to the home of the Sisters of Providence.

Irene leaned forward as they pulled up to the house, coming suddenly back to life. Her eyes followed the weathered, shingled walls up to the steeply angled Gothic roof.

"Wow. That's some place," she said. "Looks haunted."

Michelle followed Irene's gaze. The ramshackle house did look more lonely than she remembered it. Closed up. Sealed off. The mums were still on the porch, dead and brown.

Michelle saw a twitch of motion at the front window. As they parked, Adelia swung open the front door and stood at the threshold, waiting for them.

She didn't even glance at Irene as they climbed out of the car. She ran forward and threw her arms around Michelle, swinging her around with her momentum.

"Thank you for coming back," she said. "Thank you."

V

UNDER the wide, clouded blue skies, the house looked braced for a storm. Michelle realized that every ground-level window was shuttered. The upper windows were shrouded by curtains. Adelia cast nervous glances at the sea as she waited for them to reach her.

"Come on in," she said.

Adelia ducked her head as she led them inside, almost as if she were avoiding a blow. When she closed the door behind them, they stood among shadows. She gestured them into the living room.

With the windows covered it was a dim cave, with only slivers of late morning light slipping through cracks in the heavy wooden shutters. Adelia turned on a table lamp but stood outside its pool of yellow light.

"What's going on with the barricades?" Michelle asked, gesturing at the windows.

"I'm alone out here. I had to be ready in case they came after me again."

"What do you mean, 'again'?" Michelle asked. She sat down on the couch. Irene remained in the doorway.

Adelia hunched her shoulders up, her posture stiff and awkward. She watched Irene as she spoke.

"Two days after they chased us on the island, that night, they came back. There were a bunch of them this time, probably seven or eight. Maybe more."

"More what?" Irene asked, confused.

"The creatures I told you about," Michelle said.

"Yes," said Adelia. "But I closed up the house as soon as you were gone. We pissed them off. I knew they'd try to break in, to stop us."

"Stop us?" Michelle said. "You didn't know I was coming back."

Irene leaned on the doorframe, craning her neck to look over the entryway and the darkened staircase.

Adelia turned her attention back to Michelle. "I thought you would. I hoped you would."

Michelle shook her head at the rationale.

"Well, I did, after all. And I brought my cousin. Adelia, this is Irene. Irene, Adelia."

Irene left her post and crossed the room to shake Adelia's hand.

"Hi," Adelia said. "Welcome to the Sisters of Providence. Well, one Sister, anyway."

"I'm sorry, Adelia," Michelle said. "At least you're okay, though. At least you kept them out."

Adelia gave Michelle a sideways glance. "No. They got in, part-way. But I was able to stop them from breaking all the way in."

Irene laughed suddenly, too sharp. Michelle and Adelia both turned to her.

"You're both kind of crazy, you know?" she said.

Michelle stood up. "Cool it, Irene. This happened. It's happening. That's why we're here now."

"They broke in the kitchen door again," Adelia said, her voice rising.

"It's okay, Adelia," Michelle said. "Irene, would you go get the bags?"

Irene locked eyes with her for a moment, then smiled without humor.

"Sure," she said, and went back out to the car. She left the front door open behind her. A swath of daylight lit the hallway. Dust glittered in the air.

"Show me the damage," Michelle said, and walked back to the kitchen.

Sand gritted under her feet as she entered. The back door was split with a long vertical crack, as if it had been struck with an axe. Both hinges were broken now. Adelia had nailed boards across the door to keep it in place.

"When did they do this?" she asked.

Adelia paused to count the days.

"Two nights ago," she said. "I had started to think they weren't going to come."

Michelle put her arm around Adelia's shoulders. Adelia felt small against her.

"Well, you have them blocked now," she said. "And now you have reinforcements."

———————◆———————

"Your purse is still in the room you used," Adelia said as they sat on the porch in the bright sunlight. "I tidied up your notebook and stuff. I put more books up there, too. Ones I thought would help with your research."

Michelle lit a cigarette. She offered the pack to Adelia, who shook her head. Irene put out her hand, though, and lit one, too. The wind stripped the smoke from their mouths as they exhaled.

"I wish I had had the idea to go up to school before I quit, and see what they have on Ardoch and the Sisters of Providence. And on the Eliots of Boston, as you put it," Michelle said to Adelia.

"I doubt they would've had anything, Shelly," Irene said. "This isn't the kind of stuff that makes it into university libraries. Half of it is just scary stories kids tell each other. You'd have a better shot at finding things around here—local papers and local histories."

"Which I have," Adelia added.

Michelle ground out her cigarette on the dry wood of the porch and flicked the filter toward the side yard.

"It just all happened so fast," Michelle said. "I guess I'll learn it as I go."

"Yeah," Adelia said. "That's kind of how I fell into it. I was curious, I came out here, and then suddenly I was in it. The learning about it came later."

She watched the sky over the dunes.

"At least I had a few Sisters here to explain things. I'll do the best I can, but I don't think I ever learned everything that Whitemarsh and Akady knew."

"Is there any way to get in touch with them?" Irene asked.

Adelia looked at her.

"No," she said. "They're all out of this now."

———————◆———————

Michelle brought in the box of family documents from the car and carried it up to what she now thought of as her room. Adelia followed her up, and showed Irene into the room across the hall. It was a space as spartan as Michelle's, but without the sea view. It even had the same radio.

"Well, then," Irene said, looking around the bedroom.

"This was a place for getting away from things," Adelia said. "Everyone who came here just sort of...left the rest behind."

Irene shrugged and dropped her tote bag on the bed.

"I've seen worse," she said, looking at the faded bedspread and the rag rug. "Remember that dump of a motel in Seaside, Michelle? We were what, fourteen? The stains on the rug, the crappy vending machines. That was crazy."

"Yeah," Michelle said. She smiled briefly and looked past her cousin to Adelia. "Should we go to the island before it gets too late?"

Adelia squinted out the window at the bright band on the western horizon.

"We'll go tomorrow," Adelia said. "It will be too dark before we even get there tonight."

Michelle looked at Irene. "That's probably better, anyway. You'll be able to see the whole island, and we can get you up to speed on what's happened."

Irene raised her hands in front of her, palms out.

"How about we wait until tomorrow for all of it?" she said, with an edge of anger in her tone. "The getting up to speed, the island, all of it. Right now I'm tired and just want to eat and go to sleep."

Adelia's glance flickered to Michelle.

"We can do that," she said. "I'm going to heat up a pot of corn chowder for dinner. Come down when you're ready."

When Adelia had gone downstairs, Irene sank down on the edge of the bed.

"I'm sorry, Shelly," she said. "I'm tired. I'm trying."

————— ◆ —————

Irene retreated as soon as she finished her soup. Michelle went up to her room early, too, after she had helped Adelia clean up from their meal.

She pulled out the box her father had given her, and unpacked it on the bed. She wanted to be familiar with her own history before she began digging too deeply into another's.

She sorted the letters, notebooks, and photographs into piles, then sorted those piles into smaller stacks by dates. It took her longer than she thought it would. She heard Adelia settling the house for the night. She heard Irene toss restlessly in her creaky old bed. The hours ticked by. She kept getting lost in the minutiae of the collection, seeing a name or a mention of a place that made her pause. She forced herself back to a cool distance several times before the box was emptied and she was satisfied with her categories. Then she took out her own notebook and began her survey with the oldest papers.

There were only a few letters in this pile, from her great-grandfather's sister Claudia. Michelle read over the simply written missives, full of Claudia fussing at her brother, worrying over him, assuring him that yes, there would be work for him when he came to Passaic. But a passage in one letter stood out.

"I am terrible to think it, but I am glad that Gertrude is gone and that you are leaving your life up there behind you! Thomas is nearly grown, and I don't want him to suffer among all those terrible memories. She was never good to you or to your son. She was not like us."

Michelle scanned the rest of the pages, but Claudia did not speak ill of her dead sister-in-law again.

Among the loose papers was a yellowed photograph in a cardboard slip, a family portrait become a memento mori. Michelle was only mildly surprised to see that her great-grandfather, Joseph Inverno, was considerably older than his wife. But Gertrude, staring sternly out from the faded print, startled her. The wide mouth, the wide-set, light-colored eyes, the narrowed lower jaw, all showed the origin of the family resemblance.

Michelle studied the slightly blurred face of her grandfather, Thomas, as a child of seven or eight where he posed stiffly beside his mother's skirts. He looked more like his father, Michelle decided. She put the photograph back with the letters, and moved on.

The second stack she had made was larger, with letters exchanged between Thomas and his future wife. He had known Maria Boland before he left Gloucester with his father, and remained in contact with her over the next few years. They courted by post until he went back north to marry her and bring her back to New Jersey. Michelle barely remembered her grandfather. Her grandmother had died years before Michelle was even born.

Their wedding picture, safe in its tarnished silver frame, revealed a resemblance that should not have been. Marie Boland shared the same features as Gertrude Inverno, almost as if they were sisters.

Michelle slid the photograph from its frame and held it side by side with Gertrude's image.

She shook her head. As far as she had ever known, Gertrude was an orphan in a port city when she married. Her family was a mystery. If Maria and Gertrude were related by blood, it would explain why their traits were so dominant in their descendants.

The idea of inbreeding had once seemed purely academic to her, something practiced in ancient Egypt and isolated cults. But here it was, in her family, a possibility. Michelle scribbled a few notes, her handwriting an unruly scrawl across the page.

She turned next to the photo albums. Under the crinkled plastic sheets were her mother's baby pictures, her first birthday, her mother a laughing child in Maria's arms.

Tears sprang up in Michelle's eyes. She fought against the pressure to cry.

She cleared the piles onto the floor and put herself to bed. The blanket pulled over her head muffled the sobs she could not stop.

———————◆———————

Michelle woke Irene after she had washed up, and waited to go down to breakfast with her. Adelia had coffee and toast waiting for them.

"We have grape jelly or orange marmalade," she said. "Sorry it's not fancy. It's nearly time to restock the cupboard."

"Where do you go for groceries?" Irene asked. "This isn't near anything."

"There's a store in Gloucester that delivers. Which is good. I haven't had a car to use since Sister Whitemarsh left."

"How do you place an order?" Irene persisted.

Adelia looked at her blankly. "By post."

"And where is your mailbox, all the way out here?"

"Irene, what's wrong with you?" Michelle cut in, sharply. "Eat your toast and shut up already."

"It's at the corner of Ardoch Road and the main road. You passed it when you came in." Adelia downed her coffee in one long pull. "Is there anything else you want to know about how we function out here?"

Irene ducked her head.

"Look, I'm sorry. It's been a bad week."

Michelle stood up.

"Stop apologizing. Let's get going," she said.

———◆———

Adelia led them across the dunes to the causeway. She pointed out the few eggs clinging to the rocks to Irene, and explained what they were. Irene listened, impassive.

On the island, Michelle led Irene to the graves, and told her again of the larval creatures they hid. Adelia kept watch on the choppy sea.

Irene looked at the sad sunken trench, and ran her hand over the weathered sign.

"Beloved children?" Irene said after a minute. "That's what these monsters are burying here, too, isn't it?"

Adelia looked from Irene to Michelle, and down to the pitted ground. Her face was set, unreadable.

"Looks like," she said.

From the island they walked up and down the beach a short distance to see if anything strange had washed ashore. There was nothing but the usual black seaweed, the common, broken shells. With noon approaching, they headed inland to visit Ardoch.

Irene studied the shattered buildings with wide eyes and listened as Adelia described what had happened there. Irene wandered a short distance away from them as Adelia spoke, peering into the shambles.

"But why would they come this far in from the water to eat?" she asked.

"Easy pickings," Michelle said. "Many of the townsfolk were sick and easy to kill."

Irene nodded absently.

"I think I want to go lie down for a while," she said.

Adelia shrugged, and led them back to the house.

———◆———

"I'm sorry for how Irene's acting," Michelle said when she was sure her cousin was safe behind a closed door. "She had a bad breakup literally right before we came out."

Adelia plucked at the sofa cushions. "Why did she even come, then?"

Michelle sat down beside her. Dust motes drifted and spun in the dim golden air.

"We need more than just the two of us. She'll be alright."

Adelia didn't answer. She handed Michelle a new stack of diaries to go through.

"I hope so," she said. "When they come again, they aren't going to just back off. We have to be able to hold the house against them."

Michelle nodded.

"Did you read all of these?" she asked.

Adelia looked at the pile.

"Not really. I skimmed through some of them. Studying was never my strong suit."

"But you know what's in them, anyway. The other sisters must have been great story-tellers."

"They were. You would have liked them, I think. Akady especially loved the history of this place."

Michelle nodded again, flipping open the top diary.

"I'll see how well I get on without her."

———◆———

The day wound down into blue dusk. Adelia went through the rooms, turning on the lights. The shaded bulbs did little to dispel the gloom of the closed house. Michelle brought her new pile of books up to her room to study later. Irene woke up and joined them again. Her mood remained quiet, if not as sullen as she had been.

The three women made a simple dinner of ham sandwiches and coffee and settled in to eat. Even with the shutters in place, Michelle could feel the weight of the night looming over them. The boarded-up door made the kitchen feel like a trap. She reached for a second sandwich and took a bite.

"I want to get an early start tomorrow," Irene said.

"We can do that," Adelia said. "What did you want to start with?"

"No," Irene said. "I mean to get on the road."

Michelle coughed as she tried to choke down her mouthful.

Adelia looked up from her plate. "Aren't you staying? I thought you were staying?"

"Yeah," Michelle said thickly. "I'm going to be here for a while. You knew that. I thought you were going to help me."

Irene shook her head slowly. "I never said that. You know I wasn't planning on this being more than a couple of nights," Irene said. "I have to go to work on Tuesday."

Adelia looked from Irene to Michelle.

"So take the car," Michelle said. "Adelia, is that okay?"

Adelia nodded. She continued eating.

"All settled then," Michelle said. She took one last bite of her dinner, got up while chewing, and threw the rest of the sandwich in the garbage. She left Irene and Adelia at the table and headed upstairs.

Irene glanced at the door and then back at her plate. She didn't meet Adelia's eyes.

"I'm sorry about this," she said. "Michelle misunderstood."

"It's okay," Adelia said. She rose and started to clean up.

Irene crumpled her napkin onto her plate.

"I'll be back in a week to check up on you two."

Adelia didn't respond. She kept herself busy at the sink until Irene, too, went upstairs to her chilly room.

VI

WITH Irene gone, the two women settled quickly into a quiet routine. Adelia ran the house as she always had, and kept an eye on the sea. Michelle cloistered herself in her room, reading through the messy chronicles the Sisters had kept.

The published memoirs were largely puffery and repurposed folklore, suggestive of what Michelle was trying to piece together without being actually useful. She flagged passages as she dug her way through the narratives, knowing she would probably not reference them again but not willing to ignore them. The books of genuine folklore proved more substantive, if only because they did not pretend to be fact.

The first reports of the creatures that haunted this shore were from the 1880s, when fishermen began to describe strange bodies in the sea: *"Mr. Samuel Ternley says that when he was a young man it was not uncommon to see what he referred to as 'not seals.' These creatures might be mistaken for seals once, he said, but not again. 'When you see it the first time, the only thing you can think it might be is a seal. But it isn't, it isn't anything you want to be able to name. The next time you see one, you know to look away.'"*

There were also odds and ends clipped from newspapers and pasted into a scrapbook, gossip and society news, which had been annotated in a fine and spidery hand. Beside a short, cryptic wedding announcement was an elaboration longer than the clipping. *"In March of 1891, Miss Evelyn Cash-Warren was wed to a man whose name was not recorded, although witnesses later attested to the propriety of the contract. The groom was described afterward as exceedingly tall and slim, and with a distinct foreign air. No further details about him were revealed, before or after the marriage. Mrs. Cash-Warren (?) herself withdrew from society immediately following the wedding, with only rare contact with family and former associates over the next several years before becoming* completely reclusive. She died and was buried in 1897. There is no record of the fate of her husband. It is believed the couple died without issue."

The Sisters had thought this marriage important. Michelle made her own notes about the annotations, her own hand not nearly as neat.

The real treasure of information lay in the journals that Letitia Eliot—Michelle assumed it was her, from the now-familiar handwriting—had compiled. Sister Eliot had an eye for detail, and the presence of mind to have organized her observations. As Michelle read through them she realized that the journals were compendiums of what must have been a slew of other notes and musings, recopied here to corral them by topic for other eyes than Eliot's own.

Michelle stopped making her own scratched notes and began to bookmark Sister Eliot's.

"I hesitate to call the creatures mer-folk—they are more akin to eels, I think, being black and elongated, though still man-shaped.

"They come out of the sea as they get older. They can breathe air then. Their colors change, too. They start to look more human. But they're not, not even close. They hunt, on land, for food, and other things. They mingle with human company at times.

"I have not been able to determine if there is any difference between the sexes, but the eggs they lay appear to be fertile.

"From what I have observed first-hand or have been able to deduce from other sources, the creatures go through three distinct life stages—egg, larva, and adult. In the larval stage they seem normally to burrow to reach sources of carrion on the island, but they may also remain hidden in shallow water in protected areas and scavenge from what washes up on the tides. After sufficient feeding they encyst, and emerge from eight months to a year later as the amphibious, mature form that has been reported in other accounts.

"However, I believe there is a fourth stage that is occasional, and depends on circumstances I have not been able to define. At times, I believe the adult creature will shed its skin and emerge as something resembling a human female. These false women attempt to integrate into human society. They will take a human male as a husband and bear him children."

Michelle read the passage again. Even among such strange musings it made no sense.

"The creatures breed, and their normal-seeming, half-human offspring breed in turn, and still the mongrel creatures retain a human look. They for all purposes are human, since they breed only with *humans once they have taken on the false, human-like form. But despite the generations of interbreeding, despite the human blood intermingled with the amphibian, the offspring will still seek to return to the sea."*

Michelle fumbled with the book as she reached for another bookmark, and the journal fell from her lap. It landed on its cracked spine, and fell open to reveal a bookmark placed by another reader.

Tucked into the pages was a surprisingly crisp photograph of a dozen women and girls standing in a line in front of the house Michelle stood in, back when it had been grand and well-maintained. From the women's dresses and hairstyles, Michelle guessed the photo was taken before the first war. She examined the faces that squinted into the long-ago sun. Two of them, a woman's and a girl's, resembled her own, her mother's, her grandmother's.

It shouldn't be.

Michelle turned the stiff picture over, but all that was inscribed on the back of it was, "August, 1915."

She flipped through the journal, hoping to see where the photograph had been glued into place, hoping for a caption.

She found instead where a page had been torn out, and then another, a few pages further on. Several had been removed at the back of the journal, after the entries had ended.

She stuck the photograph back in to mark a missing page and carried the journal down.

———— ◆ ————

Adelia was out on the wide porch, making her daily check on the shutters and doors. She had rebuilt and reinforced the back door, and had secured plywood to the windows behind the heavy wooden shutters. The house was a dark cavern inside, but it was as secure as Adelia could make it.

"I found something," Michelle said, pulling Adelia's attention away from her defenses.

Michelle opened the journal and showed Adelia the photograph.

"This says it was taken sixty-three years ago," Michelle said. "Do you know who these women are? What their names are?"

Adelia looked at the old image, running her finger over the figures. Michelle pointed to one of them.

"Her, for example," she said.

"My guess is that it's probably Alma Phillips, and that would be her daughter, but I don't really know. Those are the only names I really remember."

Michelle held the opened book out.

"There are pages missing. I think this picture was on one of the pages that are gone."

"I never noticed that," Adelia said. "But it's been a long time since I looked at any of the books."

"I'm kind of surprised that wasn't part of joining the Sisters," Michelle said.

"It might have been. But not when I joined," Adelia said. "By then it was just a few of us, and there were things to be done. Besides, I told you I was never was one for reading."

Adelia looked back at the photograph, and then at Michelle.

"You look a little like them," she said. "Maybe you're related. Wouldn't that be funny?"

Michelle put the photo back into the book.

"Yes," she said. "A funny coincidence."

Michelle hugged the closed book against her chest.

"I think you're going to need to read some things, whether you like to or not," Michelle said. "Then we can talk about how funny it might be."

VII

MICHELLE handed Adelia a mug of coffee and sat beside her on the porch steps, flipping through her notebook without looking at it.

"Done?" Adelia asked.

"Not even close," Michelle said. "I have to digest what I've read so far before I can take anything else in."

Adelia sipped at her coffee. Michelle watched the steam rising from the mug, wreathing Adelia's face. Adelia watched the water.

"Why don't you go after the eggs?" Michelle asked after a while. "Get them before they burrow?"

Adelia took a deep breath. "I don't know. I never thought about it. Sister Akady used to say that we should let nature kill as many eggs and hatchlings as it will before we risk ourselves by drawing the creatures' attention. But she never said not to. We just didn't."

Michelle looked back over the pages in her hands.

"I think we should go for the eggs."

Adelia shook her head.

"Why bother?" she asked.

"Because," Michelle said, "they're just floating there. No digging needed. We can kill more than if we waited, and that means fewer to dig up."

Adelia gestured out over the dunes with her coffee cup. "We'd be exposed on the causeway."

"Think about it, Adelia. It's no more or less dangerous than going to the island. I think the Sisters went for digging rather than scooping eggs out of the sea because of their skirts getting in the way."

Adelia laughed.

"Besides," Michelle added. "We're the Sisters now. We can try other ways."

"That's true," Adelia said, standing and flinging the rest of her coffee at the sandy ground. "I've been used to holding on to what was, out here. Never gave a thought about being able to change it."

———————◆———————

They got out of the house as soon as the sky brightened enough to let them see.

The beach was barren this late in the fall. The great swell of the sea still held on to some of summer's warmth, but the best of it had faded. The rising sun spread an apricot glow across the horizon. Adelia walked a few steps ahead of Michelle, her fist tight around the handle of the spade. Michelle carried her garden fork over her shoulder like a rifle.

They stopped at the rise to the causeway. It was just past low tide. The sea before them was flecked with light from the rising sun as it began its slow creep up the beach. The women stood together and watched the coming waves. No dark heads broke the surface. No long, slick bodies slipped along the rocks.

"We have to be fast," Adelia said. "We can start nearest the island and work our way back toward shore. At least that way we'll be facing in the right direction if we have to run."

Michelle nodded, and led the way up onto the causeway.

They peered over the side as they went. Eggs nestled in the hollows of the rocks, rolling gently with the sway of the waves. There were fewer than Michelle remembered from her first visit. A scattering of empty cases still clung to the strings that connected them, flapping like torn leaves in the water.

Michelle reached the edge of the island and turned in a full circle, making sure there was nothing moving toward them in the sea. She looked up at the sky as well. It would be a beautiful day.

"Ready?" she asked, and Adelia nodded.

Michelle reached down with the rake and dragged a short chain of eggs up onto the causeway top. They fell out of shape without the buoyancy of the water, their covering slime picking up grit from the sandy pavement. Adelia stepped forward and sliced each one with the spade, twisting the flat blade to tear them open. Dark, half-formed things seeped out from their shredded casings. Michelle looked away, and moved on to the next cluster of eggs.

The women moved swiftly back and forth down the causeway in a destructive rhythm, leaving an uneven trail of ruined things behind them. They both scanned the sea every few minutes, but there was nothing to see in the waves lapping in the breeze.

"I don't know why we haven't drawn any attention so far," Adelia said.

Michelle hooked up another slimy clutch. When she glanced up, she realized they were more than halfway back to shore. She smashed the eggs with the rake, not waiting for Adelia.

"I don't know. Just keep going," she said, peering into the water to find the next string of eggs.

They moved steadily and reached the end of the causeway again without any sign of trouble from the sea. The sun had become a pale bright disc in the sky. Waves stretched higher up the beach. Michelle checked her wristwatch.

"Just going on eight o'clock," she said. "Not bad."

Adelia planted her spade in the sand and leaned on the handle.

"I thought they'd come to stop us," she said. "It's always been a mad dash to crush the larvae and run before they can reach us. This doesn't feel right."

Michelle shrugged. "Maybe they've moved on. Maybe they know they can't stop us."

Adelia shook her head. "No. This has been their breeding ground for ages, since before Sister Eliot founded the Sisters of Providence and found them. They wouldn't just give it up now. They came after us, what, three and a half weeks ago? A month? They're still here."

Michelle gently took Adelia's arm and tugged her toward the house.

"We can't make them come after us if they won't. Let's go get some breakfast, rest up, and see what the day brings. Maybe we can make some progress on the island, too, if the creatures still stay away."

Adelia looked at her blankly.

"You don't really get it yet. They aren't just ignoring us."

She pulled the spade from the sand and dragged it behind her as she headed up the beach.

"They'll come. When they're ready. So we have to be, too."

VIII

THE following Sunday morning they heard the rumble of Michelle's Beetle chugging toward the house. They went out to the porch to greet Irene as she pulled in.

"Hi," Irene said as she got out of the car. "Here I am, as promised."

Michelle hugged her cousin tightly.

"Thanks," she said. "How are you doing now? Are you better?"

Irene waved at Adelia where she stood at the bottom of the steps.

"Yeah, I'm better," Irene said. "Look, I told Matt to come out here, too. He's a little bit behind me."

"Why?" Michelle asked. "What about being broken up?"

Irene shrugged and surveyed the empty landscape around the house. "Because it's creepy out here, and I thought he would be good to have around."

Michelle looked at her. "This wasn't an open invitation."

"You didn't ask about inviting me, either," Irene replied. "But here I am. Now help me with my stuff."

Michelle looked into the car.

"How much stuff did you bring?" she asked.

"Enough," Irene said. "Look, I'm sorry about how I left. Now I'm here for the duration."

"Okay," Michelle said, then took one of Irene's bags and lugged it up to the house.

———◆———

"So, how are you two holding up?" Irene asked, strolling into the living room after Adelia. She looked around at the blankets piled on the couch and the papers and books spread out on the floor and coffee table. "Looks like you're cramming for an exam."

"Sort of," Adelia said. "Catching up on some things."

Irene bent to pick up a photo from a stack of loose papers. She studied it for a minute, her mouth quirking into a smile.

"Is this your other gramma? Your dad's?" she asked Michelle.

Michelle looked at the picture in Irene's hands. "Yeah, that's her."

"She was so young," Irene said. "I remember meeting her when I was small, when we came down to visit."

"Yeah," Michelle said. "She's been gone a long time."

Adelia began to gather up all the documents into a tidier pile, and stacked the books neatly on the table. When she finished, she picked up one of Irene's bags.

"Let's get your stuff upstairs," she said.

——————◆——————

"Matt's here!" Irene yelled from her room. Michelle joined her at the window in time to see Matt crest the rise, his Duster's exhaust loud and in need of repair. He went too fast for the sandy path, and slid when he hit the brakes. His tires kicked up the dirt beneath the sand.

Irene jogged down the stairs and straight out the front door to meet him. Adelia followed her closely. Michelle reached the porch as Matt swung open the car door.

"Well, you're on time," Irene said.

"You said to give you two hours."

Irene looked away. "Yeah. Thanks."

Matt got his bags from the trunk and stood there uncertainly as Michelle and Adelia assessed him. At last Michelle stepped around her cousin. "Hi, Matt," she said, holding out her hand. "I'm Michelle."

"Hey," he said, shaking her hand once before letting go. "Irene told me about you."

"Same," she said. "This is Adelia. This is actually her house."

Adelia waved, keeping her distance.

"Matt is Irene's boyfriend," Michelle said, choosing the simplest answer. "She asked him to come and help if he can."

Adelia shrugged. "Okay," she said. "We have room."

She turned away and went back into the house. Michelle stepped back, hanging awkwardly between Matt's car and the porch steps.

Irene stood beside Matt, looking at her feet.

"Are you going to show me in?" he asked her.

Irene glanced at his luggage.

"I didn't know you were planning on staying."

"You said things might get weird. Did you really think I was going to just stop in and say hi, and head back out?"

Irene shook her head.

"Look, I'm glad you came. Come on in."

———◆———

After a makeshift lunch, Michelle pulled Irene aside and pressed a thick fold of bills and her car keys into Irene's hand.

"Do me a favor," Michelle said. "You've seen the state of the pantry. Take Matt and go to one of the big groceries in Gloucester this afternoon. Get us plenty of food, stuff that will last."

Irene looked at her, then at the money in her hand.

"Wow. We're not trapped here," she said.

"No," Michelle answered. "But we might not want to leave for a while. Or have anyone else come in."

"What do you think is going to happen?"

Michelle put her hands into her pockets. "I don't know. We've been going through all the records here and figuring out stuff. How much of it is real, I don't know yet. But it makes some sense out of what I've seen already."

"Are you going to tell me about it?" Irene asked.

"Well, yeah," Michelle said. "But right now I need you to go get groceries."

Irene shrugged.

"I'll see you later then."

———◆———

Michelle found Adelia in the kitchen, sitting with her hands around a mug of tea, staring at the solid panel where there had once been a door with a window.

"I sent them off to get us supplies," Michelle said. "When they get back we can give them the short version. Right now, I'm going to go for a walk to clear my head a little."

Adelia shifted to face her.

"It's been too quiet," she said.

Michelle sat down next to her, and put her hand on Adelia's arm.

"There's nothing we can do about that," she said.

"I know," Adelia said, moving her arm. "It's just the sitting and waiting that wears me out."

Michelle patted the table.

"Me, too," she said. "I'll be back in a while."

She pushed back her chair, gathered up her coat and her camera, and headed out toward the beach.

———— • ————

The breeze was sharp with salt as Michelle crossed the dunes. She stood still for a moment, letting the cold air wash over her. All around, the long grasses and scrub rustled and moved. The sea before her glittered in the afternoon sun. The island seemed to hover over it at the end of its rocky tether.

She took her camera from her pocket and took a snap of the beach and the causeway. Then she made her way down to the smooth sand above the waterline and trudged north along the shore. A thin line of black seaweed marked where high tide had reached. Broken shells studded the sand and crunched under her feet. She stopped periodically to take pictures of the rocky shoreline as it stretched away, and of the pines and bayberry scrub that fringed the dunes. Except for the shriek of gulls floating high over the sea, it was silent beyond the constant rush of the water and the wind.

She wasn't sure how far she had gone. The house was out of sight behind the sweep of long grass. Her footprints seemed to stretch for miles.

As she turned to go back, she saw the shape breaking the rhythm of the water. She froze. The dark oval head lifted and cut through the waves, moving toward her. It stopped before the waves broke against the shore, floating there, watching her. It was close enough that she could see the wide, luminous eyes, the wide, lipless mouth, the pale iridescence of its face. This time it was not a shock to see those features.

A second head rose above the waves beside the first. With almost surreal detachment she pulled out her camera and snapped pictures until the roll was done.

The first creature opened its mouth, let out a high, bubbling whistle, and disappeared under the water. The second silently followed.

Michelle ran as fast as she could back down the beach, her coat flapping around her, her hand clutched tight around the camera.

IX

"I don't know why they didn't attack you. Why they're watching you," Adelia said, putting a glass of water and an ashtray on the table in front of Michelle. Her voice was tight with tension. "Promise me you won't go out by yourself again, though."

Michelle lit a cigarette and waved it in the air in frustration. "I won't," she said. "But we should try going out again, together, to see if anything else happens."

The crunch of tires on sand sounded from the front of the house.

"And then what?" Adelia asked.

The front door creaked as it opened, and Irene called out for them to come help unload the car.

"Maybe we can figure out what they want," Michelle said, rising to answer her cousin. Adelia opened her mouth to reply, then shut it and only shook her head.

"We will," Michelle said as she left the kitchen.

As she stepped out onto the porch, Matt smiled up at her.

"I think we did okay," he said. "And we brought back the change."

Michelle laughed stiffly, and took the heavy box Irene handed up to her. She led the procession back to the kitchen. Matt made two more trips before everything had been brought in.

"We may be here a while," Irene said, grinning. "And even if we're not, this won't go to waste."

She started unpacking the boxes of groceries, revealing a feast of canned ham and fruit and tuna fish, coffee, tea, honey, powdered milk, dried beans and rice, pasta and eggs and peanut butter, jelly and bread. Paper bags held two gallons of fresh milk and an assortment of apples and pears. Another box had frozen orange juice and chopped meat, whole chickens and pork chops.

Adelia began filling the freezer with the meat. "This is crazy," she said. "I should've asked for ice cream."

"Guys, I have to show Irene something," Michelle said. "We'll be back down soon."

She tugged at Irene's sleeve and pulled her upstairs.

"There's still stuff in the car," Irene said as they climbed the stairs. "Soap, shampoo, toilet paper, all that. I got you a couple of packs of Marlboros, too."

"Great," Michelle said. She led Irene into her room and closed the door.

"I need to talk to you," she said. "About what's going on, about what I've found out so far."

"Okay," Irene said, sitting down on the edge of the unmade bed.

Michelle brought out the picture of her great-grandfather and his wife.

"This was my mother's side of the family, her grandparents," she said. "My great-grandmother died before my great-grandfather moved away from here. But when I think about what my dad said about him, I don't think my great-grandfather had any idea about his dead wife. I don't know if my grandpa did or not."

Michelle handed Irene a second picture, of Michelle's maternal grandparents.

"Look at them, the grandmas. They weren't related as far as we ever knew. But look how they look alike."

Irene studied the photographs.

"Yeah, they do. Maybe they were family, after all. You look like this grandma. Like your mom."

Michelle took the pictures out of Irene's hands and put them on the nightstand.

"My dad always told me that my great-grandmother died a long time before my great-grandfather came to New Jersey. That he was so lonely after she was gone that he saw something, imagined something. And that's what scared him away from the sea. But I think what happened is that her real family came for her."

"What are you talking about?" Irene asked sharply.

A light knock sounded on the door. Adelia opened it without waiting for an answer.

"Wait, your father told you this?" Irene continued, ignoring the interruption. "I thought you said it was your mother's side."

Michelle paused for a moment before she answered, making eye contact with Adelia. Adelia closed the door behind her and sat beside Irene.

"It is," Michelle said. "But she would never talk about it. My dad treated all her stories as family history, and passed them on to me after she died. But he never really considered them, because they weren't his. He never thought them all the way through. I think my mother did. And that's why she wouldn't talk about it."

Michelle pulled a bent cigarette from the half-crushed pack in her pocket and lit it. She blew out a long streamer of smoke.

"I think my version makes sense, but there's no one to ask."

Adelia scratched her head with both hands, making a cloud of her hair. She smoothed it down again.

"I didn't know we were going to talk about any of this now," she said. "We were still hashing out what happened today."

"What happened today?" Irene asked. "What did I miss? We weren't gone that long."

Adelia ignored her. "Does any of what you think match up with any of the records here? I mean the interviews and experiences, are they like what your grandfather believed?" she asked Michelle.

"In parts? I don't know. My family stories could have been in one of the sailor memoirs. The rest just makes sense to me, even if I can't prove any of it."

Adelia sat very straight, and spoke softly. "Did I hear you say you think your grandmother's real family came for her? What does that mean?"

Michelle leaned over her to put out her cigarette. "My great-grandmother. I think she was somehow connected to these creatures."

Irene looked shocked. "That's just nuts," she said.

Adelia was quiet. She gazed levelly at Michelle, picking at her fingernails. Then she sighed.

"You know what you're saying, right?" she said.

Michelle paused. Before she could respond, Irene stood up.

"Matt's still downstairs," she said. "He needs to hear this, too."

She opened the door and headed down, calling Matt's name as she went. Adelia rose as well, and gestured to Michelle to follow her.

"She's going to tell him anyway," Adelia said. "Might as well get it over with."

Matt had waited in the kitchen when the women disappeared. Now Irene stood behind his chair, waiting for her cousin to come in.

"Okay," she said when they were all in the room. "Apparently some strange things happened here while we were out shopping. We need to know, since we're in this now."

Adelia pulled out a chair and sat down across from Matt. Michelle leaned against the refrigerator with her arms crossed over her chest.

Irene stared at Michelle. Michelle looked away, and started to explain.

"All right," she said. "So after you two left I went out for a walk. By myself, on the beach."

"Foolish," Adelia said, half under her breath.

Michelle cast her a sharp glance.

"And two of the creatures I told you about, Irene, came up to the beach to look at me."

Irene shook her head and turned away.

"You know," she said, "when you first told me about what you thought you saw, I was willing to go along because I thought there was a good chance you had seen it wrong, and that we could figure it out. That's why I came back."

"We are figuring it out, Irene," Michelle said. "But it's weirder than I thought it would be."

"How so?" Irene said. "How weird are you going to get with this? Do I need to let your dad know what you're talking about?"

Matt reached behind him and took Irene's hand to guide her into a chair. "Come sit," he said to Michelle.

He looked around at the women.

"Can someone please tell me what's going on?" he asked. "Irene didn't do much by way of explanation."

Adelia and Michelle looked at each other, until Michelle gestured at Adelia to start. Adelia shrugged.

"Do you know anything about the Sisters of Providence?" she asked Matt.

"Just the usual stories. I came out here a couple of times when I was a teenager, but we never made it past the ghost town."

"Close enough," Adelia said. "The short version is, there are monsters in the ocean near here that look sort of like humans, and prey on humans when they can. The Sisters of Providence have been fighting them for years. Now I'm the last one. Well, and Michelle, now."

Matt looked down at the table top before meeting her eyes.

"You believe in sea monsters?" he asked cautiously.

"I don't have to believe in them. I've seen them. I've defended this house from them. That door behind you. They broke it down and I fought them off."

Matt blew out a stream of air in a long, low whistle, and glanced sideways at Irene. She avoided his eyes.

Adelia turned to Michelle. "Now it's your turn," she said.

Michelle tapped her fingernails on the tabletop in an uneven rhythm.

"We showed Irene where they breed, on the island. She's seen the eggs," Michelle said slowly. "If she had stayed longer, we would have shown her more. All the evidence the Sisters kept."

She drew a deep breath.

"But today I was...observed...by two of the creatures when I was out on the beach. They didn't try to come after me. They just watched me, and made noises. I took pictures of them."

Irene shook her head again.

"Shelly," she said. "You showed me some stuff, the graveyard, things floating in the water. I know you believe in these monsters, but what have you really seen? Maybe it was a seal, or a clump of seaweed. Something normal. Not the monster story you want it to be."

Matt leaned back in his seat.

"I didn't know it was going to be like this when I said I'd come up, Irene," he said.

"There are pictures," Michelle said, her voice rising. "From when this place started. There are women then who look like my grandmother, my great-grandmother. Me. That's what the creature I saw looked like too. I can show you when I get the film developed. What about that?"

Irene reached for Michelle's hand, and held it tightly.

"It's likely they all had family from the same little village in Portugal," she said. "And you filled in that face on whatever it was you saw. Just please think about it. It makes more sense than what you're trying to make it be."

Michelle hung on to Irene's hand. "I'm not crazy," she said.

"No one said you were," Irene said. "But what you're saying is. I think you're overthinking what you read, and what you saw, and you're getting overwhelmed."

Adelia stood up, her shoulders hunched and tight, and started pulling various ingredients from the refrigerator. She opened up cabinets and got out bowls and pans. She turned on the oven to heat.

"She isn't overwhelmed. These things are real. I've seen them too," she said. "You can write us both off, but you'd be wrong."

She opened up a loaf of bread and began to tear up pieces into the bowl.

"Irene, I don't really care what you think. Or you, Matt," she said. "I know what's going on here, and what we are trying to do."

She reached into the freezer and pulled out a package of chopped meat that had not had time to freeze. She ripped open the wrapping and dumped it into the bowl as well.

"Right now, I am going to make meatloaf for dinner. I don't want to talk about this any more tonight."

Matt got up and pushed his chair in. He gripped the back of it.

"Okay," he said. "No more tonight. We're here, so let's make the best of it. I'm going to wait in the living room. Please call me and I'll set the table when you're ready."

He smiled to keep the peace, and walked down the hall. Irene looked at Michelle and Adelia before she went after him.

Michelle held her head in her hands and drew a long, shuddering breath.

"I'm sorry," she said to Adelia's back. "I'm not doing this very well."

"We'll be okay," Adelia said over her shoulder. "We just have to stick together."

X

MICHELLE and Adelia sat together on Michelle's bed, the dark room frosted with moonlight. Michelle smoked one cigarette after another, slowly, aiming the exhaled smoke toward the narrowly opened window. Cold air sliced through the gap. Adelia flipped the edge of the bedspread over her legs.

"I thought I'd be able to count on her," Michelle said quietly.

Adelia sighed.

"More people leave here than stay," she said. "It's always been that way. I was surprised when you came back."

Michelle was silent, her gaze fixed on the dark sky. She rearranged herself on the bed, leaning back against the headboard.

"I don't think I could have stayed away," she said at last. "I feel like I fit here. Even though it's not...healthy for me."

Adelia picked up the cigarette pack from where it lay on the bed, turning it over and over in her hands. She tapped one out, put it in her mouth.

"You still don't smoke," Michelle said.

"No," Adelia said. "Give me the matches."

As Michelle sat forward to hand them over she stopped, turning toward the window.

"Do you hear that?" she asked.

Adelia shook her head. Michelle stretched across the bed to reach the window, pressing her face to the cold glass, trying to see past her reflection. She pushed the window up and leaned out into the night. Michelle watched the sea. Dark shapes moved among the rocks on the moon-flooded beach. More shapes were already crossing the sand, moving inland. She pushed herself back from the sill.

"They're coming," she said to Adelia.

Below them, something clattered and scrabbled on the porch.

"They're here," Adelia said, her eyes wide.

They heard the squeal of the front door opening and then the slam of it being shut. From the living room, Irene screamed.

Michelle ran from the bedroom and thundered down the stairs.

Irene was at the front window, staring at the glass as it rattled in its frame from the scratching and slamming on the barred shutters. Through chinks in the heavy wood Michelle could see slivers of pale, quasi-human faces. She closed her eyes and pulled Irene back. The sounds from outside were maddening.

"Where's Matt?" she asked, giving Irene a slight shake.

"I'm here," he said from the hallway.

"Are you okay?" Michelle said, turning to him.

He nodded. "We heard noises out there, and I opened the door to look, and they came at me... I don't know what they are," he said.

"Sea monsters," Michelle said.

Adelia came down the stairs at a run. She looked from Matt to Michelle.

"We can't let this happen again," Adelia said. She opened a closet set into the space beneath the staircase and began pulling out possible weapons. She handed Matt one of two baseball bats. Michelle snatched up a claw hammer, and handed Irene a hand axe in a worn leather sheath.

"Irene, go into the dining room and watch the windows. If anything starts to break through, scream and we'll come," Adelia said. "Matt, you take the front door. Michelle, take the kitchen, check the door, make sure it's secure."

She hefted the second bat. "I'll watch the living room windows. Same all around—if they start to break in, scream."

Matt stared at her for a second, stunned, before moving forward into the entryway with the baseball bat held before him like a sword, taut and helpless. All around them was the sound of wood cracking beneath the creatures' assault. The noise they made was relentless as they scraped across the encircling porch and dug at the boards that kept them out.

Irene followed Michelle down the hallway and took a deep breath before going into the dining room alone. Michelle thought she heard the squeal of metal tearing at the back of the house. She feared hinges being pried loose, the repaired back door failing.

As she entered the room she saw the back door was intact. She felt a brief moment of relief before she froze at the sound of splintering wood coming from the cellar. She heard the creak and snap of the wooden steps under a multitude of clawed feet. She heard the slither and chatter of the creatures as more and more of them struggled upward. She heard the screech of the lock giving way, and then the heavy cellar door shuddered and cracked under the weight of bodies pressing up and clawing at it. In seconds the door fell in and the creatures surged into the kitchen.

Michelle screamed, and raised her hammer, but the creatures swarmed toward her, filling the narrow entryway to the kitchen. Michelle swung at the closest one and sank the hammer's claws into the thing's shoulder. It shrieked like a gull and flopped backward, but the others shoved its body out of the way and massed around her. She couldn't get her arm up, couldn't swing the hammer again. The creatures pressed close to her, grabbing her limbs in their clawed hands and dragging her toward the barricaded door.

She screamed again, wordless and rough, as the creatures battered down the door and hauled her resisting body out into the cold night. She lost her footing on the steps, but the creatures only stumbled and yanked her along.

When they reached the dunes, some of them dropped down onto the sand and writhed like snakes, making for the sea. Michelle kept screaming, a high wail that broke as the creatures hustled her into the booming surf and pulled her under with them. Beneath the cold water, she couldn't scream any more.

XI

MATT ran out into the eerie new silence, but stopped where the tongue of light ended.

"Michelle!" he bellowed, but got no response.

"Come back in," Adelia said. She looked stricken. "We can't be sure they're gone."

He shook his head. "No. I want to look around first. Do you have a flashlight?"

Adelia rummaged through a messy drawer until she found one. She pushed the switch and it shone with a dim yellow light.

"Not sure how long it will last," she said.

"I'm just going to check around the house," Matt said.

Irene stumbled in, her face a bloodless mask.

"Don't go," she said.

Matt ignored her and stepped into the dark.

He followed the unmistakable mass of tracks down the side of the house until he reached the outside entrance to the basement. He played the dull light over the bulkhead doors, and let out a low whistle.

The doors were steel, but they had been forced up far enough to break the sliding bolt lock, and thrown back to let the slippery creatures in.

Matt tightened his grip on the baseball bat as he shone the flashlight into the black space. The heavy smell of salt and seaweed washed up the cellar stairs to meet him. He stepped back to catch his breath.

A light snapped on in the basement.

"Matt?" Adelia called from below, her voice slightly hollow from the space around her.

"I'm here," he answered.

Adelia came up the slippery cement steps to meet him.

"Anything?" she asked. He shook his head.

"Okay. Close the doors so we can lock them somehow."

He pulled the heavy doors shut, lowering the second door as he descended the steps. It was like closing a tomb.

"Here," Adelia said, holding out a coil of rope. "We can thread it through the hinges for now, and just hope for the best until we can do something better."

As he pulled the rope tight and tied it off, he glanced at Adelia.

"We need to get out there and look for her. How many flashlights do you have? And do you have a gun?"

"Stop," Adelia said. "They're gone. I don't have a gun, and it's too dark. We'll have to wait for morning."

"That might be too late," he said.

Adelia rubbed her eyes. "It's probably too late now. But we have to hope, don't we?"

"Guys?" Irene called from the kitchen. "Could you please come up and help me with this door?"

——————— ◆ ———————

The three of them took turns keeping watch through the night, but beyond the noise of the sea and wind there was nothing.

When Matt came into the dark kitchen at five A.M. he found Adelia already there, seated at the table with a cup of coffee in her hands, staring at the back door. She glanced at him, then turned away.

"Irene has been tossing and turning since she came up. She's washing up now. I don't think any of us slept," he said.

"Dawn's a ways away yet," she said. "Another hour, hour and a half, until we can try to track her."

Matt pulled out a chair and dropped into it, exhausted. "We already know they took her into the water, don't we?"

Adelia's nose reddened and she blinked back tears. "Then I want to recover her body," she said.

Matt slumped back in his seat.

"We don't know she's dead, Adelia. She may have gotten away from them. We'll look for her. I just don't have a lot of hope that we'll find her."

Adelia slurped her coffee. She wouldn't look at him.

———◆———

As the sun rose, they armed themselves again and walked to the causeway. The tide was still low enough for them to cross it. Adelia looked over the sides to see if any new eggs were strung along the rocks, but only strips of seaweed clung and lifted on the waves.

The island was empty when they reached it. The sea spread out calmly around them, glossed with gold by the rising sun. A line of clouds spread just above the horizon. Adelia walked to the oceanward edge of the island, across the burial ground. She shaded her eyes and looked to the water for any sign of Michelle.

"This is the graveyard," Irene said to Matt. He nodded, his eyes on Adelia where she stood above the waves.

"Let's look on the beach," he called to her. "There's nothing here."

Adelia didn't move at first. Then her shoulders sagged and she joined them on the walk back to shore.

As they stepped down from the causeway, Adelia stopped. She looked up at the sky as the morning brightness was swallowed by clouds. Without the sun, the air grew quickly chill.

"Which way do you want to go first?" she said.

Irene scanned the beach in both directions. "Maybe that way?" she said, pointing south.

"All right," Adelia said. "Come on."

"Wait," Matt said. "I don't want to split up, but we can cover more ground if we do."

Adelia stared at him, as if she didn't quite understand him. Irene wrapped her arm around Adelia's and leaned against her. Adelia blinked, and slowly nodded.

"Irene and I will go north, then," she said. She looked at her watch. "It's ten to seven now. It looks like we might get some weather. Let's walk out until eight, and then meet back here."

"Sounds good," Matt said. "If either of us isn't back on time, we go looking."

"Yes," Irene said. "Be careful."

Matt smiled thinly at her, and headed down the beach.

Adelia tapped her baseball bat on the hard sand and, still arm in arm with Irene, started walking in the opposite direction. Irene clutched her coat close around her neck against the seeping cold. Their breath misted in the damp air. They did not speak. Adelia kept her eyes down toward the sand, but Irene scanned the waterline with a stubborn hope.

They had walked only twenty minutes, and gone nearly a mile, when Irene cried out without words and jerked at Adelia's arm to point at a crumpled shape a few yards up the beach.

"Michelle!" Adelia shouted, tearing herself loose from Irene's grasp and running to her.

Michelle's body lay face up at the tideline, splayed like a fallen doll. Her half-buried hair swirled around her head, clouded with sand and flecks of seaweed. Her sodden clothes were torn, and sweeps of wet sand covered her legs. A string of six black eggs wound around one arm, each of the casings crushed and empty.

Adelia dropped to her knees beside Michelle's limp body and brushed the crusted sand from her face. A deep gouge across her cheek opened like bloodless lips beneath Adelia's fingers. Adelia gasped. Michelle's face and neck were scored with scratches, and her hands showed pale bite marks on her fingers and wrists.

Irene stumbled to a stop behind Adelia and coughed out a sob.

"Oh my God," she whispered, over and over.

Adelia ignored her. She turned Michelle's head toward her and opened her mouth. A clot of seaweed fell out onto the sand. She tugged at Michelle's shoulder to pull her onto her side and began patting her back as if Michelle were a baby.

Nothing happened.

Adelia struck her harder, the flat slap of her hand on wet fabric a sharp counterpoint to the slush of the waves.

Suddenly Michelle convulsed and retched. Foam and water spilled from her mouth. She choked, gasped, and retched again.

Adelia slapped her back several more times, then rolled her onto her belly, careful to keep Michelle's face turned to the side, out of the sand. She grabbed Michelle by an arm and stood up.

"Help me!" she demanded, and Irene took Michelle's other arm. They dragged her up the beach onto the dry sand. Michelle heaved from their manhandling and brought up more water.

"Go find Matt," Adelia said, scraping Michelle's hair back from her white face.

Irene nodded and ran back down the beach.

After an unmeasured length of time, Adelia heard the thud of footsteps behind her. She did not turn around. She kept her eyes on Michelle's drained face, her half-lidded eyes, the film of spit across her mouth that trembled as she breathed.

"Matt," Adelia said, finally standing, short of breath. "I can't lift her myself. Get her back to the house."

XII

MICHELLE became aware of a comfortable weight spread across her body, and of soft light shining through her closed eyelids. Beneath the warmth and light, she ached. She became aware of the mattress beneath her and how it pressed uncomfortably against her shoulder blades and hips. She wanted to move her legs, but the idea of it was exhausting. Her chest felt too heavy, as if a stone lay on her. She struggled against the ugly sensation and drew a deep, painful breath. She heard herself wheeze as she exhaled.

Beside her, someone stirred.

"Shelly?" Irene's voice murmured from somewhere close by.

Michelle opened her mouth, but her tongue was dry and clumsy. She dragged air in again and tried to speak, but her breath eased out like a sigh.

"Shelly!" Irene said again. Michelle felt her cousin's lips against her ear. "Can you hear me? Can you answer?"

Michelle struggled against the immovable weight of her own body. She opened her eyes to a blur of light and color, the smeared shape of a face. She willed herself to speak.

"Yes," she made herself slur. "Hi."

She heard Irene move abruptly, the creak of wood, the squeak of a hinge.

"Matt! Adelia! She's awake!" she heard Irene shout from a distance.

She closed her eyes again. The pain in her chest settled into a slowly pulsing rhythm as she breathed. She let herself drift, even as Adelia and Matt ran up the stairs, even as Irene clasped her damaged hand in her own. As her three friends gathered close to her, to witness her survival, Michelle let go of the world and fell back to sleep.

———————◆———————

"It was terrible," she said. "They were trying to take me away, and they didn't care how they did it."

Adelia put her hand on Michelle's arm, leaning toward her. It had taken Michelle days to reach the point where she would speak about it.

"What did they want?" Adelia asked. "Why did they take you?"

Michelle shook her head. She didn't want to say it. She looked out the window at the grey sky. The thin curtains moved in a draft. She was comfortable under the quilts, tucked into her bed. She didn't want to relive the cold.

"They took me under the ocean with them," she said slowly. "They kept me there. I saw the sun rise, from underwater. But I didn't drown."

"You were lucky," Adelia said fervently.

"No," Michelle insisted, moving her arm away. "I didn't drown because I was breathing in the water."

Adelia shook her head. "You couldn't. You can't. You went through so much before we found you, you had to be dreaming it."

Michelle turned her face away.

"I wasn't dreaming. I could breathe. And I thought after everything you've seen, all the things you've shown me, that you would at least hear me out."

Adelia sat quietly, twisting her hands together. Michelle could almost feel her drawing into herself. She kept her eyes on the sky to ease her frustration, and resumed her story.

"I thought I was going to die. I thought they would eat me, and I only hoped they would kill me first. But they brought me with them. The rocks of the Baby Island go far, far out underneath the sea, and there are tunnels and caves carved into the rock. They lead up, some of them, toward the cemetery. But most of the cemetery tunnels start much higher up, on the edge of the island. Not everything is connected."

She paused.

"They took me into the caves. There is a whole web of them running into each other, spreading out underneath the sea floor. But they kept me here, near the island.

"They didn't tell me any of this—they couldn't. The things don't speak. But being in those caves, I just sort of knew how they moved about, and how wide their territory was. It was like an instinct instead of actual knowledge.

"And even though it was dark in those caves, I could see. Not details, but enough to know where the openings were, and where the creatures were. There was sort of an aura around things, but it wasn't something my eyes were picking up. It was just *there*, I could just *see*."

She paused, collecting her thoughts.

"Breathing was like that, too. At first I thought I would die, because it hurt so much when I couldn't hold my breath any longer and drew in the first lungful of cold water. I don't know how to explain it. It was like being crushed. It felt like my chest was full of iron, it was so cold. I was so cold, but I couldn't get warm with my lungs full of cold water. But I didn't drown."

Michelle plucked at a thread on the blanket, pulling out the stitches. She turned back to Adelia.

Adelia struggled to meet her eyes.

"This is why my great-grandfather left Gloucester. This is why my mother needed to be in the ocean."

"I don't understand," Adelia said.

Michelle sighed and gathered her strength.

"Did you ever wonder why the creatures had never attacked the house before? Not like they did when I first came here, or that last night?"

"No," Adelia said quietly.

Michelle shifted under the covers, trying to sit up higher. Adelia helped her lean up, and tucked a pillow behind her shoulders.

"When the Sisters would leave, where would they go?" Michelle asked.

Adelia looked at her as if she was not sure she understood the question.

"Home. They went home."

"They went home to the sea," Michelle said. "Like my family did."

Adelia shook her head. "No. That's not true. If it were true, why would we be here to fight them?"

"I don't know," Michelle said. "Sister Eliot figured it out, the connections, the interbreeding, but she didn't see the whole picture. And the later Sisters, the ones you knew, they didn't either. They got it wrong. The creatures aren't going to attack the house again. Not now that I know."

———— ◆ ————

Michelle crossed the dunes slowly, leaning on the garden fork like a cane. It was her first time out alone in nearly two weeks. It was exhausting. She could smell the storm coming in on the cold wind, the suggestion of early snow. She tugged her hood down over her forehead and kept going.

The grasses hissed and flattened beneath the wind, and she leaned forward against it. The waves frothed before they broke and scrawled up the beach. She walked forward until her boots grew wet from the grey water rushing around them. She stood there, and waited.

Eventually, six sleek shapes slid up through the shallows, their heads lifted above the waves. She watched them as they manipulated a great soft thing drifting in the water between them, slumped in the shallows by its own mass. They nudged and cradled it until it bumped along the rocky base of the causeway, until it caught on the rough surface and adhered to it, unspooling into dark, knotted ribbons.

Eggs, Michelle realized. New eggs.

One of the creatures slithered up onto the sand and looked at her with unblinking liquid eyes. It opened its wide mouth and trilled out an undulating whistle before turning and swimming back into the sea. As the six creatures disappeared back under the water, Michelle wet her lips and let out a long, wavering whistle in answer.

She could not tell if they heard her.

———————◆◆———————

Michelle dozed on the living room sofa, bone-tired but not entirely asleep. Irene came in and sat on the floor beside her.

"Shelly? You awake?" she said softly.

"Mostly," Michelle said, not opening her eyes.

"I have to talk to you."

Michelle raised her head enough to look at her cousin.

"I think I should go home. Not immediately. But pretty soon."

Michelle propped herself up on one elbow. "Is it Matt?"

"No," Irene said. "He's actually being very not-pushy. He's trying."

She shifted her legs beneath her to better face Michelle.

"I've been staying to make sure you're okay, and I think you're there," Irene said. "You've got some kind of purpose here that I don't get. But I don't have to." She paused. "It's only twenty miles back home, but it's like being on another planet out here. It's not for me."

Michelle sighed, and smiled.

"You always go your own way. I've always admired that about you."

Irene burst into tears, and wiped her face on the hem of her shirt.

"Now I'm an idiot," she said, starting to laugh.

Adelia came in and handed Michelle a mug of tea. She looked at Irene trying to compose herself.

"What did I miss?" she said.

"Irene is going to be leaving us again," Michelle said.

"Oh," Adelia said. "Oh."

"It's okay," Irene said, grabbing Adelia's hand. "I'm only going back to Ipswich. I'll be your person on the outside."

"Matt's going too?" Adelia asked, her face beginning to crumple.

"Going where?" Matt said from the doorway.

"Leaving. With Irene," Michelle said.

"I didn't realize you were going to tell them yet," Matt said to Irene. She shrugged. Matt looked at them, sheepish.

"No. I was thinking of staying here with you two for a while longer, if that's okay," Matt said. "Until you're back on your feet, Michelle. I started to read some of the notes, your notes, and—I don't know. We'll see how things go. If it's okay with you."

Michelle sat up, blowing on her tea to cool it. She sipped at it, watching Irene. Irene would not look at Matt.

"It's quieter here in the winter," Adelia said at last. "They're quieter. We can repair the house. I usually clear the island and then walk the beaches. They sometimes lay eggs and burrow along the bay. But not always. Not every year." Her voice faded away.

"The eggs don't matter," Michelle said. She reached for Adelia's shoulder and squeezed it. "We'll be okay here, the three of us. For now."

———— ◆ ————

Michelle bundled up with blankets over her coat and retreated with Adelia to the porch steps. Behind them, in the house, she could hear Irene and Matt speaking, arguing, saying their goodbyes. Michelle sighed.

She leaned back against Adelia's knees and closed her eyes. She was glad Matt had offered to stay, for all that it troubled Irene. Her convalescence was taking far longer than she had thought it would. It was a strange injury to come back from. Her wounds had closed and scarred over, but her chest still ached from breathing in the sea, and the air tasted strange on her tongue. She still felt as though she had been beaten against the rocks like laundry, leaving nothing but bruises and sore muscles.

It felt good to do nothing but sit in the long yellow wash of the setting sun and listen to the gulls and the waves, and let the jumbled pieces of her life fall into place.

Adelia let her hand fall on Michelle's shoulder. Michelle covered it with her own, warming Adelia's chilly fingers.

———— ◆ ————

November 15, 1978
Dear Dad,
I just wanted to let you know that I'm all right and everything is fine. I won't be home for Thanksgiving this year. Please don't be a martyr about it, though—go to Aunt Peg's.

There's no phone up here, so I'll call you on Saturday morning when we go into town for groceries and fill you in better then.

I did want to say thanks for giving me all of Mom's stuff. It really helped me sort things out. I understand her in a way I couldn't when she was alive. I understand myself in a new way, too.

I love you, Dad.
I'll talk to you on Saturday.
Love,
Michelle

About the Author

ERICA Ruppert lives in northern New Jersey with her husband and too many cats. She writes weird horror and dark fantasy, and her work has appeared in magazines including *Unnerving*, *Lamplight*, and *Nightmare*, on podcasts including PodCastle, and in multiple anthologies. When she is not writing, she reads, bakes, and gardens with more enthusiasm than skill. This is her first book.